A Tale From The
West Pennine Moors
Overlooking The Old Market Town
Of Chorley, Lancashire, England

She's Missing

By K. E. Heaton

Other books from the same author:

Tales Of Entrapment – A Trilogy

Book 1 – Death On The Algarve: Eyes Of The Water

Book 2 – Uncle Joe's Revenge: Death On The Cut

Book 3 – Devoid Of Guilt: A Portuguese Harvest Of Death

Text copyright © 2019 K. E. Heaton
All rights reserved

This is a work of fiction. Names, characters, businesses, places, events and incidents are either the products of the author's imagination or used in a fictitious manner. Any resemblance to actual persons, living or dead, or actual events is purely coincidental.

Dedication

I dedicate this book to my wonderful wife and kids.

Table Of Contents

Chapter 1 9

Chapter 2 21

Chapter 3 31

Chapter 4 41

Chapter 5 51

Chapter 6 61

Chapter 7 75

Chapter 8 83

Chapter 9 93

Chapter 10 101

Chapter 11 111

Chapter 12 119

Chapter 13 129

Chapter 14 137

Chapter 15 145

Chapter 16 155

Chapter 17 163

Chapter 18 175

Chapter 19 183

Chapter 20 195

Chapter 21 203
Chapter 22 211
Chapter 23 221
Chapter 24 231
Chapter 25 239
Chapter 26 249
Chapter 27 267

She's Missing

K. E. Heaton

Chapter 1

1976

The outlook from the old farmhouse was spectacular. Located high up on the West Pennine Moors and overlooking the ancient market town of Chorley in the distance. It had a commanding field of vision extending out towards the Lancashire coast.

Fred Smith had purchased the house in 1956 when Tom was only four years old. He'd spent the next ten years renovating the place from top to bottom whenever he had a spare moment. As a self-employed builder in the years that passed he became more and more successful and therefore in a better position to push on with his own enterprise and complete the project. The end result was remarkable, an impressive five bedroomed property with an indoor pool and garaging for at least four cars, quite an achievement for a council house kid. He moved the family in, in the summer of sixty-six on the same day that Geoff Hurst hammered in the fourth goal at Wembley which sealed West Germany's defeat and Kenneth Wolstenholme famously said. "Some people are on the pitch… they think its all over… it is now!"

And so it was.

Fred could now enjoy his life's ambition and move to the hills in a lovely part of the county still near to his work and friends but far away enough from his childhood roots. Compared with his mates therefore Tom had it relatively easy. When he left school the same year he began to work for his dad but it was evident that he wasn't well suited to the hard physical work his dad had endured previously so he went on to college and then university. Subsequently he became a draughtsman and designer and a valuable member of the team, or so he said. He still lived in the family home so when Fred and Mavis decided to buy a second property, a holiday home in Spain, often Tom was home alone, but never for very long.

Strangely, somehow on this particular evening, it appeared as if the sun had been granted a stay of execution. It was ten o' clock and still the magnificent blushing beast would not be tamed. Defiant right up till the end. Denying the close of play until eventually mercifully the fiery brute was smothered and slipped away beyond the horizon leaving behind it a wonderful sky of pinks and orange.

But then suddenly, as if she'd been waiting patiently in line, a warm fragrant wind hurried forward and began to dance cheekily between the swaying drapes.

"Oh… what a relief." Said Susan as she turned her pretty face towards the French doors. "That breeze is lovely."

"You're not kidding." Tom sighed. "I can almost breath again.

"Yeah…" Susie whispered. "But will we get any sleep tonight… that's the question?"

"Well..." Said Tom wishfully as he cast his mind back to the previous nights lustful encounter. "… I do hope not."

"NO…!" Susie insisted. "No… definitely not…not tonight, I have to work tomorrow Tom… for God's sake, it's too bloody hot."

Tommy didn't answer. He didn't need to. She knew what he was thinking. He was a rich kid with a great tan a handsome bastard and he always got what he wanted. With his thick black hair combed straight back from a high forehead, noticeably long and hanging down onto his shoulders. She wouldn't refuse him. How could she, he was the best catch in town and all he had to do was to slip his shorts off once more and soon she'd be climbing all over him. He also reckoned that he'd managed to ply his very seductive guest with more than enough liquor during the day and by now was fairly convinced that her feigned inhibitions were non-existent. No one else had ever refused him, how could they? He reckoned the answer was quite simple really… she was just playing hard to get.

But little did Tom Smith actually know Susie Fraser.

Yes she appeared more reluctant than on the previous evening but he was still convinced that he could have her again and again if he so wished.

Susie however had decided on just the opposite, she would reject his advances out of hand, and that was something Tom Smith wasn't used to.

It was nineteen seventy six and the United Kingdom was in the middle of what the weather forecasters had described as the driest, sunniest and hottest summer since records had begun. Only a few places in Britain had received half of their average seasonal rainfall and extensive fires raged uncontrolled in more remote parts of the country. Widespread water rationing was essential, public standpipes an everyday sight and emergency hospital admissions increased day by day. In fact it was estimated that at least two per cent of the deaths recorded during the summer were directly related to the heat.

Hardly surprising that Tom found her so desirable. Susie was drop dead gorgeous with a slim hourglass figure and big beautiful boobs. Her shoulder length hair was jet-black, thick and shiny, a profusion of unruly curls rebellious and disobedient. They magnified her shameless beauty, a fascinating face that captivated most men at the first glance. It had everything that girls wanted, large brown eyes, a luscious mouth, youth, symmetry and high but not excessively high cheekbones. As one of Tom's friends had described her, she was "A drink on a stick."

As Susie sprawled out on the couch enjoying the fresh night air she wore only two articles of clothing. A thin cotton blouse she'd bought off Chorley market the previous Tuesday and a pair of skimpy knickers allowing her to retain at least some semblance of decency. As she'd insisted all day, it was just too bloody hot to wear anything else. Susie wasn't particularly tall but as she stretched out and rested her lovely bare feet across the armrest, she did look quite slender. The more she stretched the more athletic and leggy she appeared. Her actions, negligible as they were, had not gone unnoticed. Susie's host raised himself to his feet very slowly and sidled over towards her.

"Listen Tom." Said Susie quite angrily. "… Don't get any more ideas… we've had a great weekend… but that's it… do you understand?"

"Yeah… yeah. I understand." Said Tom quietly. "Anyway I'm off to bed then okay… night… night."

"Night…" She said coldly now more determined than ever that she was sleeping on the couch and definitely not in his bed. "… I'm leaving early."

"Okay…" Said Tom trying his best to hide his frustrations. "… Give us a ring… eh?"

"Yeah… sure." Said Susie half-heartedly. "I'll see you later."

She lay back and closed her eyes thankful at least that Daddy's boy appeared to have finally got the hint. When he got back to his bedroom he'd soon realize that Susie had already packed her bag and moved her stuff out. When he was tinkering with his car earlier in the day she'd gone back to his room, stuffed all her belongings into the hold all and hidden the bag downstairs ready for departure. She'd jumped at the chance to spend the weekend with him, why wouldn't she? He was a good-looking guy and he had made a point of asking her as opposed to one of Susie's other notoriously decadent friends. There were plenty of other girls that would have jumped at the opportunity. However she'd now come to the conclusion that he was odd, very odd… creepy almost. She'd driven up there on Saturday afternoon after a short spell in the office. There were those in the office that just couldn't help them selves and were intent on finding out what Susie was up to. So… suspicious of being followed she'd taken a round about route in order to shake off at least one car that appeared to be shadowing her a little too closely.

She even considered for a second or two whether it might even be her mum and dad following on behind, the vehicle in question remarkably similar to her dad's old powder blue four door saloon.

But then finally when she got there everything seemed okay though as the weekend progressed she became more and more disillusioned with the pretty rich boy in the big house. She had consented to have sex with him on Saturday night and submitted without question. At the time helped along by copious amounts of alcohol she was probably more up for it than he was, but then afterwards she wished she'd put up more resistance. Perhaps she'd acquiesced a little too easily and the thought now occurred to her that he believed that he owned her like everything else he surveyed around him. He wanted to flick his fingers and for her to respond to whatever he had in mind. When she thought about it, she remembered her mother's reaction when she'd told her that Tom Smith had invited her over for the weekend.

"Yes… go." Said her Mum. "… You'll be okay there love… hob knobbing with the rich and famous… he'll look after you."

Susie's Mum had always been supportive unlike her dad. Pat Fraser had always tried to see the good in people and ignore the flaws but as everyone knew she'd made a bad choice with her partner. Susie's Dad Bob had more in common with his youngest daughter. He was an ex-serviceman and fell-runner and no doubt that's whom Sally got her love of exercise from.

Susie however disliked the smug way that Tom had glared at her once they'd done it, too self-assured, over-confident and not in the least bit grateful. He should have cherished her instead of using her. Susie hated herself for letting him have all his own way… she felt cheap. On Sunday morning her first inclination had been to cover up and not put further temptation in his way, but didn't see why she should have to, especially in this heat, and come to that she intended to teach him a lesson, make him want her even more. She wasn't going to sleep with him again, ever… not even if he begged her. It was a defiant plan of action but not without its dangers.

Suddenly Tom reappeared a glass in either hand.

"I've made us a nightcap." He announced confidently. "…It's a peace offering. It's just a brandy… it'll help you sleep."

"I'm alright thank you." Said Susie icily. "... I've had enough drink for one day."

"Just wanted to make things right... I've really enjoyed having you here... I'm sorry for being... you know... too pushy! Anyway I better get to bed."

He positioned one of the drinks very careful onto the coffee table before exiting back through the big wooden door closing it behind him very quietly on his departure. Susie lay there motionless for a long time. The windows were still open allowing a feint breeze to meander gently mercifully between the several large pieces of tasteful country furniture that Tom's mum had chosen to decorate her beautiful home. Mavis had a good eye, she was a natural homemaker and she spent Fred's money very carefully but very wisely. She'd chosen furnishings with vibrant red orange and gold colors that everyone agreed were perfect. Needless to say, Tom's dad never got involved. As far as he was concerned he just made the money and Mavis spent it for him. Eventually Susan got to her feet a little unsteadily secured the windows and doors and then drew the curtains too, aware perhaps she was ready to doze off but still conscious of the remoteness of the property and the opportunities it presented to those on the wrong side of the law. She'd worked at "Gladrights" the Estate Agents for the past three years since leaving high school and knew all too well the lengths that some homeowners went to on the West Pennine Moors to keep their properties secure. It was a wonderful place to live but occasionally it did attract unwanted visitors. It wasn't unknown for a gang from Liverpool or Manchester to target a particular dwelling or farmhouse on the hills and make off with thousands of pounds worth of money and jewels especially during the summer months. There had been certain incidents involving intimidation and even violence. The perpetrators had several escape routes available to get themselves off the moors. If challenged or once they'd completed their robbery they could head back down towards Chorley and the M61 motorway. Or could just as easily drop down into one of several other North West towns, Blackburn and Darwen or possibly Horwich and Bolton. Often by the time the police arrived the culprits were long gone.

Susie was exhausted, she grabbed the quilted throw in her left hand and dragged it unceremoniously from the back of the couch until it covered her from head to foot then fell back instantly into a horizontal position. With the drapes completely closed the room was now lit exclusively by a solitary ornate standard lamp in the corner discharging the faintest of light. Suddenly a warm eerie ambience appeared to wrap itself around her, it wasn't scary but it was slightly spooky. She listened intently for a while to all the strange noises that the old house had to offer, trying to figure out an explanation for each sound. Strange but on the previous evening when she'd been in Tom's bed she hadn't heard anything at all apart that is from their own puffing and panting as they'd thrashed about between the sheets. After that and the disappointment she'd felt about Tom's reaction to it all Susie had simply turned away from him curled up into a fetus position and gone straight to sleep. There was however one thing she did remember very clearly, he never held her and cuddled her like she would have wanted. It was unforgivable… how on earth could anyone behave like that?

"I am." She thought. "… A woman scorned."

Now when she wanted to doze off Susie found it impossible. There were just too many disruptive thoughts racing through her head, keeping her awake and not allowing her to settle. It suddenly dawned on her that she hadn't cleaned her teeth nor had she been for a pee, yet again, which made it two nights on the run that she hadn't bothered to do either before bed. The only logical explanation she could offer herself as to why she didn't need the loo was due to the hot sticky weather. As her younger sister Sally, two years her junior always said when returning home after her daily run, her clammy unsavory odor permeating the house to everyone's disgust. "She'd sweat buckets."

An hour later the room was stifling, the coverlet had been discarded in a crumpled heap on the floor and Susie was laid back spread-eagled on the couch barely able to draw breath. Realistically regardless of the security considerations there was no option, she simply had to let some air in.

Raising herself up she staggered across the room but then immediately crashed headfirst into the solid hardwood coffee table before eventually reaching the drapes.

"SHIT… Fucking bloody shit." She cursed angrily as she drew back the curtains unlocked the doors and threw them wide open.

"For Christ sake." She mumbled to herself again as she rubbed both knees enthusiastically in a vain attempt to subdue the pain. "You know what Susie girl? It was a big mistake coming here ... you're a complete idiot!"

Susie stood for a while between the open doors uttering yet more profanities but nevertheless enjoying the gentle breeze and staring out over the fields. She liked the view and she loved the house but there was one thing she'd decided without question... she didn't want anything else to do with Tom Smith and his family and she was never ever coming back. In fact she was still tempted just to cut and run immediately, get dressed, get back in her mini and head off into the sunset. Common sense however had to prevail. If she arrived home in the early hours intoxicated as she obviously was there'd be hell to play. Susie's dad was a light sleeper, as if anyone could really sleep properly in this heat and more than anything else she just couldn't face the inevitable inquisition.

She decided to leave the doors wide open make her way back to the couch and have one last attempt to try and sleep. Feeling her way carefully this time negotiating the furniture with outstretched hands she reached out and touched the large brandy glass that Tom had left for her. Amazingly the damned thing hadn't been toppled when she'd hit the table on the outward journey and appeared intact.

Susie didn't give it too much thought really. Instinctively, impulsively and very stupidly she raised herself upright, lifted the glass to her lips and gulped down the sweet fiery liquid in an instant. Almost immediately she slumped down onto the couch and fell fast asleep.

Chapter 2

It was very early and very bright when Susie first opened her eyes. In fact the whole room was aglow… and ridiculously … her immediate thoughts were that she'd left all the lights on, and that she needed to jump up quickly and turn them all off.

But then… as she came to her senses, Susie realised suddenly that she was wracked with pain, not in any one particular place but literally… all over her body. Feeling anxious and irritable as she pulled back the cover in order to swing her legs across and subsequently stand upright. She inadvertently brushed her right thigh with the palm of her hand, a spontaneous action that made Susie wince and pause for a moment with some concern, alarmed at the clammy touch of her skin. In fact Susie's flesh appeared pallid…bloodless almost and alarmingly waxen. It was chalky, white in color and disturbingly… not dissimilar to a piece of dead meat one might see swaying gently from the overhead rack in a butchers cold room.

But worst still… as she placed her feet on the floor… it occurred to her that she was without question… about to vomit.

Most of the puke came straight up and out over her arms and feet and narrowly avoided the coffee table but undoubtedly staining Mavis's beautiful carpet in the process as Susie wretched loudly and uncontrollably. Susie slumped forward, head in hands… she became increasingly worried. She was weak and drowsy and most definitely more dizzy than she had ever felt in all her life, and most distressing of all, was that she could… not… remember… a…single… thing…

Somehow, for some strange unknown reason, the previous days events had been consigned to oblivion.

Susie's blouse and her knickers were uncomfortably wet, yet this was little more than a nuisance compared to the calamity that now besieged her.

Instinctively she dropped to the ground, acutely aware that she was in no fit state to do anything, but realizing above all else that somehow in some way… she just had to get out of that house. If necessary… she was quite prepared to literally crawl out, having already decided that she would do whatever was needed to get down off the moors and make her way back in to town.

And that's exactly what she did. Unable to get to her feet Susie trawled around the floor on all fours grabbing anything that belonged to her, the remainder of her clothes, sandals and the hold all she'd hidden surreptitiously earlier in the day. Driven by an overwhelming fear either real or imaginary, she didn't know. But it was exactly that… the not knowing… it terrified her!

Susie staggered to the car, her sticky fingers fumbling with the keys, her lovely bare feet increasingly cut and bruised on the tiny shards of gravel that carpeted the huge driveway. But then once again she stumbled and went sprawling face down onto the shale as she reached the vehicle. In desperation, stretching out and with a super human effort shoved the key hard into the lock and in the same movement dragged the door wide open to make possible her escape.

Miraculously the Mini started first time and as Susie slammed her right foot down as hard as she could and the car zigzagged down the drive towards the open gates, momentarily she gazed up at the rear view mirror as that bastard rich kid exited the house completely naked, and began the chase. Their eyes met for a brief moment, until Susie turned away, too aware that what she needed to do now was to concentrate on her driving and put as much distance between herself and Tom Smith before he'd time to do anything about it.

The little car sped off quickly down the hill. Susie hanging on with grim determination as it bounced through a huge pothole at the side of the road, its tiny wheels colliding with the rough edges of the country lane. Speeding around the first major curve the back end began to slide but instinctively she stepped on the gas and the vehicle straightened out of its skid. Swinging yet again into the next bend Susie threw the steering wheel hard over to her left as the tires chewed up huge clumps of dry earth from the roadside, launching them skyward high into the air and tainting if only for a short time, yet another clear blue cloudless sky.

Meanwhile Susie's host had concluded his pursuit, he watched with keen interest as the automobile disappeared into the dust. Rocking precariously from side to side he was completely unaware of the blood trickling between his toes. His bare sweaty body glistening in the early morning sun, a prolonged blink of disapproval and she was gone.

Even though the streets were empty when Susie reached the outskirts of town, she made a conscious decision to reduce her speed. She had no clear idea of what she intended to do but the one thing she didn't want was any unwanted attention.

She would sooner or later have to change her clothes and get cleaned up but for the present she wanted to do nothing. Susie pulled up on a small quiet car park near to the A6, very close to the Leeds Liverpool Canal. A location she'd been to previously, with another guy, late last summer. They'd kissed and cuddled, but that was all, and she hadn't been back since … until now, that is.

Now things were different, a lot different. This time she was completely shattered, she felt hunted and worst of all she felt violated.

The question was… what exactly had happened up on the moors?

Susie scoured her memory for thoughts… anything… anything that could give her a clue in order to help her make sense of her predicament. She could vaguely recollect driving up to the house on Saturday afternoon, but after that, nothing. After that… it was all a complete blank.

It was a daunting prospect.

She's Missing

If Susie went along to the Police and said she'd been attacked, molested or raped, she felt sure they would respond in a proper manner and investigate her allegations thoroughly and sympathetically. But, if she didn't really know what the hell had happened… and she didn't. The boys in blue might not be so understanding and word might soon get round that she was a drunk, irresponsible and a complete slapper.

Susie's Mum would be heartbroken, her dad mortified. She'd never live it down … how could she?

"No…!" Susie whispered very gently to herself as she sobbed uncontrollably. "…Say nothing girl… just keep your mouth shut. It never happened."

Susie waited until well after seven when she knew that both her Mum and Dad would have left the house and be on their way to work. She parked up as quickly as she could and made her way indoors before any of the neighbors had a chance to see her. She had less than two hours to scrub herself clean, get dressed ready for the office and make herself look every bit as lovely as she always did.

If nothing else… she was confident about one thing.

If she kept quiet about her visit to Tom Smith's big beautiful house on the moors, and what went on there. She was certain that he would do exactly the same. Why on earth would he draw attention to himself? … The guy was a weirdo… and one day she would get her own back.

Susie had no idea how she would do that and didn't have a clue how long it might take her, but somehow one day… she would get her revenge!

Susie lived in a modest semi, a short distance away to the main entrance of Chorley's crown jewel Astley Park with its famous seventeenth century stately home and its own Victorian walled garden. As a kid she'd spent many happy hours in the park only a few minutes walk away and even now she still loved going there. Her Mum and Dads house was nothing on the grand scale of either Astley Hall or Fred Smith's huge property, but still nevertheless, it was comfortable and somewhere the Fraser's called home.

As Susie slammed the front door behind her she collapsed in the hall, her bag and belongings strewn across the floor in a chaotic jumble. And it was then she realised the one thing she'd forgotten as she'd exited Tom's house.

"Oh God…!" She screamed. "My bloody shoes…!"

The kitchen door at the end of the hallway swung open very slowly at the same protracted speed that Susie raised her head. She stared towards it with some trepidation anxious to know who might have heard her outburst and praying above all else that it wasn't her Dad.

"So…!" Laughed Sally. "As she popped her red sweaty face around the door frame. "I take it you've lost your shoes then have you Sis? … How come?"

"Get lost." Said Susie instinctively. "…Its none of your business."

"Let me guess." Insisted Sally. "…You've left them at Tom Smiths haven't you?"

Susie glared at her younger sibling. It was a look of contempt that Sally recognized immediately, she'd seen it lots of times before.

"Well don't worry." Said Sally sarcastically. "…You're in good company."

"What…?' Shouted Susie now increasingly irritated with her little sister's nosiness. "…What are you on about… at all?"

"You…" She said defiantly. "You've left your shoes behind… that's what Oliver Cromwell did… remember?"

"I've not a clue what you're talking about."

"Yes you do!" Sally argued. "We've both heard that story enough times. … 1648… when Cromwell stayed over at Astley Hall. He was in such a hurry to get out of there… he left his boots behind."

"That's really helpful." Susie muttered disparagingly as she dragged herself up. "…Thanks!"

"Are they your work shoes?" Said Sally.

"Yes… they're my bloody work shoes." Snapped Susie. "… And I've nothing else to wear… and you."

She added. "Have you been out running again... you stink?"

"I stink...!" Laughed Sally as she stepped forward. "God... take a look at yourself... you're the one that stinks Susie Fraser... and not only that... you look like shit!"

Susie bent over precariously and one by one picked up each of her belongings.

"I've not got time for this nonsense." She shrugged dismissively. "Some of us need to work."

"Was he good in bed?" Asked Sally suddenly, a knowing wanton look etched across her face, her hands fumbling nervously, a distinctive fluorescent green hair bobble popping in and out between her fingers.

"What...?" Susie replied angrily. "... See... there you go again with stupid meaningless comments. I'm not listening... get out of my way now."

"And if I don't...?" Sally retorted.

"You will!" Susie said convincingly. "... Otherwise I'll knock the seven bells out of you. I might be shattered, but I'll still floor you. ... I've done it before." She added. "And I'll do it again... NOW MOVE!"

Sally shifted to one side to let her pass. She watched Susie climb the stairs and waited patiently until big sister had all but reached the landing before calling out for one last time.

"When Sarah went to Tom Smith's house." She shouted. "They got crazy drunk and did it loads of times."

Susie tried not to answer, reluctant to show any interest at all in what had been said. But then eventually her curiosity got the better of her and she just couldn't help herself.

"Sarah…?" She answered. "…I don't know any Sarah."

"Yeah you do…" Said Sally sensing an advantage. "She used to go dancing at the Vic. Chocolate-colored hair, extremely tall… long skinny legs."

Instantly, Susie knew all too well whom she meant. An attractive girl with creamy-brown skin, very slim and lithe, she had bright shiny eyes and a warm irresistible smile that would turn mischievous as soon as any boys came on the scene.

"I suppose she told you that?" Said Susie.

"You bet."

"Then more fool her." Said Susie.

"Too right." Snapped Sally. "Cos after that… he dumped her!"

"Well then." Said Susie as she closed the bathroom door behind her. "… She's an idiot!"

Chapter 3

Despite earlier events, Susie appeared quite calm and sitting comfortably at her office desk, as the town hall clock struck nine o' clock. In regard to what happened up on the West Pennine Moors, on the hottest day of the year, Susie would say nothing. She had no intention of giving the gossipers anything to play with. She would keep her head down continue to work hard and hopefully in a few days time everyone would forget she'd even been there.

If Tom Smith stayed well away and Susie felt sure in her own mind that he would, then any speculation about their relationship would soon disappear. There was always someone else to blabber about. On the surface Susie was super confidant, just as she always was. Nothing was too much trouble and anything was possible.

But… under the surface it was a different story.

Inwardly Susie was troubled.

She had mixed feelings and none of them were good. She felt stupid for going up there in the first place, anger for the guy who'd undoubtedly used her and fearful of the consequences and what might happen next. For the moment at least, all these painful emotions were under wraps… although the question was, for how long…? She had no way of knowing.

"Everything alright Susan?" Said Jerry as he leaned over her shoulder at an almost impossible angle.

Susie looked up startled by her boss's sudden interaction.

"You seem a bit distracted this morning." He smiled. "…You okay?"

"Yes… of course." Said Susie quietly. "…I'm fine."

"So… how about we finish up on the details for Sunny View?" He added.

"Sunny View…?" Susie queried.

"Yeah." He insisted. "Don't tell me you've forgotten already… Mister and Missus Gaskell from Whittle. The big five bedroomed house on Preston Road… they came in on Saturday morning."

"Yeah right."…" Said Susie quite taken aback with all this sudden attention. "I'm with you…I'll get on it… straight away boss."

"Good… I'm glad to hear it." Snapped Jerry as he scanned the office like a hawk in search of yet another unsuspecting chick. "…And the rest of you, come on let's get moving. I know it's bloody hot… but it doesn't matter, we've all got work to do."

Jerry Thompson the owner of "Gladrights" was still single, a big hefty man who had just turned thirty.

When he purchased the local Estate Agents three years ago the company was on its backside but very quickly he'd turned it around and now, it was a thriving enterprise. An Ex-rugby player and a bit of a mystery, no one could understand how he'd made his money. He was a Lancashire lad dragged up on the back streets of Blackburn so knew exactly where his roots were. He was quite good-looking and rather flashy. His short-cropped hair was a warm reddish blonde and after months of extreme weather his skin was almost the same color. He had hot sticky-out eyes that were probably more than likely due to regular heavy drinking. But... when Jerry Thompson was at work he was always sober, completely focused and as the girls were well aware, very demanding. Most of them would say in private that they hated him but as yet, Susie hadn't made her mind up and Jerry seemed to sense it. He gave all the staff a rough time but when it came to Susie, he appeared a lot more protective and wasn't too hard on her like he could be with some of the others.

So... when Tom Smith came barging in later that morning with a brown paper parcel under his arm all tied up with string nice and neat, walked straight over to Susie's desk and slammed it down hard directly under her nose. Jerry was in there like a shot.

"Have you got a problem bud...?" He growled.

It was clear by the look on Tom Smith's face that he hadn't expected such a hostile reception, at least not from anyone else, other than Susie.

"I'm… I'm just returned something." Tom stuttered. "… To this young woman… that's all!"

Susie kept her head down and never looked up.

"Well…" Snapped Jerry immediately. "I guess you've done what you came to do… so now… I suggest you better leave… this young woman, as you so eloquently put it, has got work to do."

Tom wasn't used to being challenged and it took him by surprise, normally he was the one giving the orders, but this time, he was out of his depth. Jerry Thompson was a big man with a serious attitude and a reputation in town for being a bit of a bruiser.

A lot of his clients simply loved him, he was well informed very knowledgeable and offered them a no-nonsense service when it came to either selling their existing property or looking for something new. He would negotiate on their behalf and often get them a better deal than what they thought possible. It was a volatile market and pushy ambitious people like Jerry always thrived in this environment.

So Jerry hated young fellas like this. He knew all too well who Tom Smith was, and as far as he was concerned, the guy was an arrogant little shit and a Mummies boy. Fred Smith might be a self made man but his son was a parasite, and if there was one thing above all else that Jerry wanted, it was a good excuse to re-arrange this rich kids pretty face.

Tom looked flustered, he'd decided on a certain course of action but he'd not thought it through very well and obviously given no regard to Susie's boss. He was alarmed that Jerry might get physical and he might get thrown out on his ear. But likewise, he was desperate, especially in front of such a large audience, of not losing face.

"There was something else…" Tom muttered.

"Oh yeah… what's that then?" Said Jerry moving in for the kill.

"I'm looking for a flat in town." He said a little more confidently.

"Really…" Said Jerry as if he didn't believe a word of what the other guy was saying. "…And how much do you want to spend?"

"It all depends…" Said Tom vaguely. "I'm not quite sure yet."

"Well… its important." Jerry whispered sarcastically. "We'll need to know… do you want to leave me some details?"

"Not just now thanks…" Said Tom sensing an obvious exit. "I'll call you back later shall I… when I've got a bit more time?"

"Yeah… do that." Said Jerry. "…Ask for me… personally. I'll make it my business to sort you out."

It was then the laughter began, a feint sound of tittering at first at the back of the office until eventually they all joined in. Till then you could hear a pin drop, everyone listening intently to what was going on.

And… it was a sweet little girl called "Angie" who's mum had often said. "Butter wouldn't melt in her mouth" that started it all. In truth and despite her angelic appearance she had a sharp caustic wit and quite often when Jerry was out seeing clients, she had the rest of the girls in stitches. On this occasion all she did was to whisper to the girl on the next table about the current altercation and suggest that what they were actually watching was another episode of the Tom and Jerry show.

So… just when Tom thought he'd secured an honorable retreat, all the pressure was back on him and what he might dare say next. Otherwise he'd just have to leave with his tail between his legs and accept all the sniggers and the on-going public humiliation.

He turned away from Susie's desk and walked back to the door.

But then… as the performance came to an end and the curtain was coming down he stared straight back at Jerry.

"You know what…?" He blurted. "… It took me three hours to clean the bloody carpet… can you believe it?"

And then he was gone.

Jerry appeared quite exhilarated with the whole incident but then very quickly the smile disappeared from his face.

"Right… come on then." He shouted. "The shows over… chop chop back to work."

He strutted off to his own private office leaving the door slightly ajar. Sat down behind the desk and waved his hand in Susie's direction. It didn't take her long to realize that it was her he wanted to speak to in confidence. Susie placed the parcel down onto the floor and walked over. Suddenly… she was the one getting all the attention… and she didn't like it.

"Tell me Susan?" He said. Before she'd even had chance to shut the door behind her. "…What was all that about?"

Susie stared down at the cheap red plastic chair on her side of the desk, not exactly sure what to say.

"Go on… sit down." He growled. "You can take a minute to think it through… I need to make a phone call."

She slumped down in the chair immediately, so tired she'd have sat on the floor if he'd asked her and the pause in conversation was a welcome opportunity to gather her thoughts together and decide what to tell him. She avoided eye contact with any of the other girls as they walked around the main office. Most of them trying their best to act nonchalant but as far as Susie could see they all needed some lessons in subtlety and were nothing but a bunch of nosy cows.

Jerry's telephone call dragged on and on as they usually did but then finally he replaced the handset and leaned across the table.

"Well..." He said softly. "Do you want to tell me... or not?"

"Thank you Jerry..." She found herself saying. "...I do appreciate what you did... it was good of you."

"And...?" He added.

"Well that's it really..." She said pathetically. "I don't know what else to say."

"The guys a creep Susan..." He insisted. "And that's the bottom line... please... trust me. A pretty young woman like you can do a lot better. So what... the guys got money. Its how a man treats you that matters!"

"I know... you're right." She said. "I'm not interested in his money."

"That's what they all say." Said Jerry. "...But money talks."

"Not with me!" Susie argued. "I don't care."

"Good..." He grinned. "I'm glad to hear it... So... are you ready to go back to work... or do you need some more time?"

"No... I'm okay."

"Right then... I'll leave you to it." He smiled. "But if you need to talk or want me to have a quiet word with someone... you know what I mean... just say the word."

'Yeah… I will… I promise." Said Susie as she got to her feet. "And thanks again boss… I'll work through my lunch break and catch up."

"You don't have to do that."

"Its only fair." Said Susie. "… I want to."

Working through lunch was a clever move. It provided Susie with a good excuse to stay clear of the other girls and not have to explain her self. And if she wanted to, she could also claim that the boss was being hard on her for disrupting the office and that way there'd be no accusations of favoritism. To everyone at "Gladrights" that would appear to be the case but in truth Susie knew better. Susie realized when she first started working there that Jerry had taken a liking to her, but up until now, she hadn't been aware of how far he was prepared to go to protect her.

Chapter 4

The next few weeks passed without incident. Susie had tried hard to put it all behind her but there were still a lot of unanswered questions. She still couldn't remember much about the visit to Tom Smiths house especially the last night she'd stayed there and other things played on her mind.

If Tom were guilty of drugging her and worse then why on earth would he risk coming into the office that day and causing such a scene. Surely if he'd something to hide, he'd have stayed well away and come to that, why were Susie's shoes wrapped up in brown paper and tied with string, in didn't make any sense.

Any normal person would have thrown them in a carrier bag and left them by her car. But as she was well aware by now, Tom Smith was no ordinary guy.

The one thing she'd missed however was a screwed up note trapped between the layers of paper that Tom had used to wrap her shoes.

The note read….

"Hello Susie,

I'm upset that you left in such a hurry & that we didn't say goodbye. I was an idiot & I'm really sorry.

I just couldn't handle it & despite what people say about me, I'm not such a bad guy, I'm just like everyone else out there looking for someone special.

I think I've found her, that special person, but I've messed up big time & now I might never get her back.

And if you ever leave your shoes at my house again, I won't return them. I'll leave them exactly where they are… where they belong!

Tom."

Sally found the note by accident rummaging through Susie's belongings, but true to form, she never told her. It was hidden away with lots of other stuff that Susie had never seen, and never would see, until Sally was good and ready.

And then late one Thursday afternoon Susie picked up the phone in the office. Margaret the office manager had gone to the dentists and when she and Jerry were both out, it was left to any of the other girls to man the phone lines.

Hello this is Gladrights…" Said Susie in her usual brisk telephone manner. "… Who's speaking please?"

"Is that you Susan?" Said Jerry sounding hassled.

"Yes… it's me boss…" Said Susie enthusiastically. "What can I do for you?"

"I've got another viewing in twenty minutes." He moaned. "The Orchard at White Coppice… but its empty and I've left the keys on my desk. Can you get over here quickly? I've not got time to get there and back before the clients turn up… how about it?"

"Yeah of course." Susie agreed. "No problem… I'll leave straight away."

"Susan…?" Jerry added. "Don't worry… I'll give you some petrol money and… oh yeah… don't forget the keys…. Thanks!"

Before Susie had time to answer, the call had ended. Either Jerry had run out of cash or he was desperate to get out of the coin box.

Susie skipped over to his office quickly and grabbed the keys.

"Angie…?" Susie smiled. "…Can you please tell Margaret where I've gone?"

"And where's that then?" Said Angie cheekily.

"White Coppice…" Susie answered. "…Don't tell me you didn't hear all that."

"Yeah… I heard." Said Angie. "And lets face it… what Jerry wants… Jerry gets."

"What's that supposed to mean?" Susie growled.

"Nothing..." Said Angie. "But be careful... everyone knows...he's got his eye on you."

"You're pathetic..." Susie snapped. "Do you know that... pathetic?"

Angie put her head down and began to type furiously. Susie charged out of the office and ran to the car.

It didn't take her long once she'd got out of town and off the main road. Susie switched the radio on and sang a duo with Paul McCartney as she raced along the narrow country lanes. After all who could turn down the opportunity of singing "Silly love songs" with the man himself. But then finally when she pulled up outside the old cottage there was no sign of her boss at all. His blue Volvo was parked up a little further down the lane, but Jerry it appeared had gone walkabouts.

Hardly surprising really, in the height of summer White Coppice was truly beautiful. In the nineteenth century the most populated part of the old township of Anglezarke with its own cotton mill and nearby coalmines. A hundred years on however most of the scars had completely disappeared and what remained was one of the most amazing locations in the whole of Lancashire.

"Pretty... isn't it?" Whispered Jerry as he sneaked up behind her.

"What... God... where did you come from?" Susie giggled nervously. "I'm sorry boss... I never saw you."

"That's alright…" Said Jerry. "You were admiring the view."

"Yeah…it's lovely." Susie sighed gently. "I've not been up here since I was a kid."

"So… only a couple of years ago then…?" Laughed Jerry.

"No…!" Said Susie firmly. "Ten… at least."

"But you're absolutely right." He added. "Its hard to believe really, we're only a few miles from Chorley town center and the views are out of this world."

Susie stepped away from the vehicle and allowed her fingers to drift slowly through a cluster of wild flowers at the side of the track. "Its all so pretty…" She said.

"Come on then…" Snapped Jerry. "…Lets take a walk up the road and have a look around."

"But… the clients?" Asked Susie. "…They won't have a clue where we are?"

"Don't worry about them..." Insisted Jerry. "They'll find us…"

Strolling up the lane side by side towards the old cricket ground, they marveled at the splendor of this special place. A tiny stream meandering its way in the opposite direction, the sound of crystal clear water trickling along through the gardens of nearby property and the ford on the left hand side. But then almost immediately it was a row of stone built whitewashed cottages elevated up above the brook.

To the front of these houses were a number of narrow wooden bridges giving access over the brook and onto a stone flagged pathway that ran the full length of the terrace. Each cottage had its own individual path leading to the garden and the outside seating areas.

Copious amounts of tiny red roses and other trailing shrubs skirted the windows and doorways. There were over-flowing flowerbeds, the odd boxed hedge and some gardens with an obvious abundance of fresh produce. It was without question a place of serenity away from the hustle and bustle of modern life.

"I'm in love..." Susie announced suddenly. "... Its beautiful!"

"Yeah... me too." Said Jerry. "I'm overwhelmed."

The cricket ground had often been described as one of the most picturesque in the county if not the country and today was no exception. It had a bumpy sloping pitch that was quite unique and quirky but above all else quintessentially English. Not a huge ground but with several large trees dotted around the boundary, yet more old whitewashed houses close by and the West Pennine Moors looming in the background it forged a memory that could not easily be forgotten.

They walked back to "The Orchard" in silence each of them completely absorbed in their own thoughts and memories.

"So... " Asked Jerry excitedly as they stepped inside the cottage. "... What do you think... do you like it?"

"Yeah… yeah…. Its great." Said Susie. "…But I thought we were going to wait… until the clients get here."

"Come on… I'll show you round." He insisted.

The house was idyllic, a chocolate-box cottage in a perfect location.

It had a large comfortable lounge with rustic beams and a huge feature fireplace. A beautiful well-equipped oak fitted kitchen with an Aga and granite worktops, three surprisingly large bedrooms and two fabulous bathrooms. Views from every window over rolling farmland and throughout the property many rough open-faced walls to remind you of its ancient past. Outdoors at the sides and rear of the cottage were large beautifully manicured lawns with a large timber storage shed at the bottom of the garden.

"Wow…!" Whispered Susie. "… I've never seen anything quite like it."

"No… me neither." Jerry agreed. "… I've been in this business for a number of years now but this is the best most luxurious property I have ever visited…. Could you see yourself living here Susan?" He added calmly.

"Yeah!" Susie said enthusiastically. "… In my dreams."

"Well then…!" Said Jerry as he grabbed hold of her hand. "… You could!"

"What...?" Susie gasped. "... What are you talking about?"

"This house..." Said Jerry. "...If you want it... we can buy it!"

A long silence followed.

"There are no other clients... are there Jerry?" Susie demanded.

"No..." He whispered quietly. "... Only us! ... Just you and me... I love you Susan.... Will you marry me?"

As children both Susie and Sally had been very competitive, very willful and very impulsive.

If either of them saw something they liked... they just had to have it. Susie in particular loathed being told what to do but occasionally faced by an overwhelming argument and if the benefits were obvious, she could be persuaded to do something she might otherwise decline.

During Jerry's formative years on the back streets of what was a hard and grimy industrial mill town he'd picked up many skills, and he was well versed in the art of persuasion.

He too would see something he liked and would never take no for an answer. He'd known straight away when she first came in looking for a job that she was the one he wanted and now eventually he'd laid his cards on the table. He might not be the pretty rich kid up on the hill whose daddy could buy you anything at the drop of a hat, but he was a guy who knew how to graft.

And… he could offer the three things that Susie needed the most, namely loyalty, stability and above all security.

It was a marriage made in heaven.

"Yes Jerry…! Yes… Yes… Yes." I will marry you. Susie screamed loudly at the top of her voice. "… I accept!"

Chapter 5

And so... in less than six weeks Susie was married. She'd moved out of the Fraser's family home and migrated to the countryside. The day Susie left... Sally tore all the posters down and claimed the bedroom as her own.

And the bedroom was not the only thing that Sally intended to take for herself. Sibling rivalry can be a very destructive force and left unchecked can lead to untold misery.

Sally had lived in Susie's shadow for far too long and now she decided was the time to show her big sister that she would never again have all her own way.

Sally's next target... Tom Smith!

Even though many girls, including Susie, had failed to tame the rich kid living up on the hill and bring him into line. Sally believed that it was possible and she made plans to do exactly that. After all she was prettier, certainly fitter and a lot more desirable than her elder sister, or so she believed. She would get to know the guy, go out on a date with him, bed him and then when she had him hooked good and proper, she'd take him home and introduce him to all the family. Susie she reckoned... would be mortified!

It was a defiant plan of action that Sally found irresistible but it was not without its dangers.

She did some digging and chatted at length to Sarah the girl with the chocolate-colored hair and long skinny legs. She learned that Tom Smith often drank in a certain town center pub after work on a Friday evening with a couple of his dad's employees. Yates Wine Lodge, as it was known, was four steps up from the pavement, open the door and the atmosphere came rolling out at you, a direct result of decades of spilled ale and tobacco smoke. So when Sally strolled in with Anne Turner her best friend from school, it was no surprise to see Tom sat by the wall at an old wooden table, its edges scarred by cigarette burns.

Luckily, he was by himself. He had a copy of the Chorley Guardian spread out before him, ashtray to one side, brandy and coke on the other.

The girls bought a drink at the bar and sat them selves down across from where he was seated. As they chatted, they looked straight ahead ignoring him completely. The first thing Tom noticed was Sally's strong athletic legs and black nylon stockings. She wore a tight thin grey sweater that buttoned up at the front and a short black skirt. Her hair was dark like Susie's but much shorter which allowed you to see her tiny gold earrings and beautiful long neck.

She'd tried really hard to look good and by the guy's reaction, her efforts had not gone un-noticed.

Tom lowered his eyes for a few seconds then looked up quickly. Now he'd caught her peering at him over her glass as she drank.

Sally had a small face, large dark eyes and amazingly long thick lashes. She'd gone fishing in the hope of catching something really big and within minutes Tom Smith was ready and eager to take the bait.

"I've not seen you girls in here before…?" Said Tom suddenly as he got to his feet, picked up a stool and sat him self down at Sally's table. "…Where are you guys off to?"

"We're not sure yet…?" Said Sally. "Though I can't remember inviting you!"

"Can't you…?" Said Tom. "I must be mistaken then… but I'm sure you just fluttered your eyes at me… No?"

"No… definitely not." Sally insisted. "You're completely mistaken…there's so much smoke in here… my eyes are streaming."

"Yeah… you get used to that." Tom sighed. "I don't even notice it any more."

"One day…!" Sally growled. "They'll ban smoking all together."

Tom laughed. "… Yeah maybe… but not in here they won't."

As planned... Sally's friend finished her drink quickly and grabbed her bag. "Come on Sal..." She said in a hurry. "Let's go meet the others."

"No... no... don't go." Begged Tom. "Please...stay a bit longer... I'll get the drinks in... what are you having?"

"Not for me." Anne insisted as she placed her fingers over the glass... I've had enough."

"You can never have enough." Tom grinned. "...Come on... just one. How about you Sal? ... Will you have a drink with me?"

"Vodka and tonic." Said Sally. "And if my mates not having one... you can make mine a double."

"That's the spirit." Tom cheered loudly. "One large vodka and tonic coming up."

As rehearsed Anne made for the exit allowing Sally to try and work her magic, and if Tom's appearance were anything to go by it wouldn't take long, he looked quite blathered to begin with.

But then suddenly a group of girls spilled in off the street, unsteady on their feet, faces red from hours of drinking. As they neared the bar there was a lot of pushing and shoving until one of them, a tiny girl, went sprawling across the floor near to Tom. When the girl looked up and saw him she gave a cry of delight, struggled to her feet and embraced him. They both laughed out loud... old lovers reunited.

Sally shook her head in despair.

The gatecrasher looked at Sally and grinned.

"You're still a rogue Tom Smith." She said cheekily. "Is this your new one… she's very young… shouldn't she be in bed by now?"

Sally was livid.

"No…!" Sal scowled as she made to leave. "I'm not his new one… It'll take more than one vodka and tonic to get me in bed… though I doubt it would take even that to get you on your back."

Suddenly the girl appeared much more sober, squaring up to Sally and pushing her head quite hard into her face. Sally could smell the beer on the girl's breath but also her underarms and her face powder. She was just about to punch her when the girl pulled away.

"So…" Snarled the girl. "If she's not your next conquest Tom… who the hell is she?"

"She's a friend." Said Tom as he stepped between them. "…Just a friend!"

"No…" Snapped Sally. "No… I don't think so… Not now!"

And before he could answer Sally Fraser had gone.

After a short but wonderful honeymoon in Scotland the newlyweds arrived back in Lancashire. Jerry lifted Susie in to his arms and skipped lightly up the path through the old doorway and into the hall.

Susie had always kept her thoughts and feelings to herself in previous relationships but this time something was different. She'd never felt any particular devotion towards any man, and certainly not her dad. So this man "Jerry Thompson" with his big strong hands, powerful body and gentle disposition... why was he any different?

But he was.

She'd decided that people either loved or detested him and even though she'd never told him how she felt, Susie had already made her decision.

Jerry however made no secret of his love for her. He simply adored his new wife... as he would the baby as well... when that came along!

It was a pleasant enough day in Chorley on the first of September. The hot summer had given way to more normal seasonal temperatures and the sun, there one minute and gone the next, was hidden briefly between billowy white clouds that blew in across town from the Lancashire coast.

Sally stepped out into the street after yet another job interview, this latest one at a local TV rental business that needed shop assistants. It wasn't what Sally wanted but her recent exam results weren't that great and after leaving school that summer, Sally's mum was now insisting that her youngest daughter get a job. Having Sally at home all day was becoming a bit of an issue. If she'd had helped out a bit more when her mum and dad were at work, things wouldn't have deteriorated as quickly. But now the relationship had suffered and the only option was for Sally to find employment.

Sally wore black that day, a tiny dress that suggested rather than revealed her figure, but definitely one that was sure to impress any male interviewer. The problem was, she'd had to face endless stupid questions from a frumpy fifty-year old female dragon unable see the advantages of having to train up a stroppy schoolgirl, who she considered was too big for her boots.

And then suddenly… there he was… staring straight at her… Tom Smith!

He was smiling and instantly she could feel the color rising in her cheeks.

"Its a lovely day Sal." He grinned. "… And you look gorgeous… but… you don't need me to tell you that do you… you already know?"

"Is that so…?" She grinned back. "Well then… it appears that you know everything about me."

"I make it my business." He shrugged. "You see… there I was looking for the prettiest girl in town… and now I've found her… again."

"You're an arrogant bastard… aren't you Tom?" She said.

"I am Sal…" He agreed quite smugly. "…Don't know any other way."

"But actually… you're not that particular are you?' Sally laughed her eyes sparkling mischievously. "…About some of the people you hang around with?"

"Oh… I get it." Tom sighed. "…You're referring to Maggie aren't you… the girl in Yates Wine Lodge? And you know what… she is a bit earthy."

"Earthy…?" Sally protested. "That's no way to speak about your girlfriend?"

Tom reacted as if Sally's comment didn't even warrant a reply. It was obvious by his manner that what Sally had said, was not to his liking but then inevitably his arrogance got the better of him.

"Girlfriend…?' He growled. "No… you've got it all wrong love… Maggie Sutcliffe has never been my girlfriend!"

"So…!" Said Sally. "What… you've never slept with her?"

"Its none of your business." Tom snapped angrily. "But I will tell you about someone I have slept with… shall I?"

"I couldn't care less." Said Sally. "… But let me guess…some other loser?"

"Susie Fraser." He insisted. "… Your big sister… yeah… I slept with her."

Susie held his gaze. Outwardly she was calm but inside knotted with anger.

"Well… more fool her." Sally sneered. "She always did make bad choices when it came to men."

"I don't know…" Tom snarled. "I could always do for you… what I did for her."

Sally tried hard to compose her self. "…No chance." She said eventually. "You can't afford me…"

"Afford you…?' He laughed. "… Listen… let me tell you something… I can afford anything or anyone I want… including you!"

Sally moved away quickly eager to put as much distance between her self and Tom Smith as she possibly could.

"A week on Saturday…" He shouted. "…Come over… by yourself. My parents are away again. We'll have the house to ourselves… I promise you… we'll have a great time!"

K. E. Heaton

Chapter 6

That night Sally was back at home camped out in her newly acquired bedroom. If she'd had any money or even the faintest promise of a job from the TV rental company, she wouldn't have been there, but the sad fact was…she had neither.

With the volume turned up on the stereo Sally never heard anyone come in and so when her mum burst into the room without knocking it was inevitable that a serious disagreement would follow.

Sally stared at the door open-mouthed her heart racing.

Pat Fraser Sally's mum was a very pretty lady and it wasn't difficult to see where the Fraser girls got their good looks from, she had light brown hair swept up in a roll around her head just like a halo and amazing soft blue eyes. Her dresses were always plain, the severity of which suited her and she'd never worn anything frilly or ostentatious ever in her life. Pat was confident, hardworking and self-motivated and a good mother. There was however, as Sally believed, a chink in her mother's armor, one very obvious flaw and that was her favoritism for her first born child… namely… Susie.

It was something that Sally had been aware of all her life and the main reason as to why the two sisters… could never be friends.

"For God's sake." Pat screamed. "… Turn that damned thing off… now… before the neighbors start complaining. "You and I lady… we need to talk!"

"About what…?" Yelled Sally.

"You know what." Cried Pat. "… All this hanging around the house… you need to get a job… and quick!"

Sally sank back on the bed and closed her eyes.

"Sit up." Screamed her mum. "Sit up… when I'm talking to you."

"I've tried… for loads of jobs." Sally insisted. "But… the truth is… nobody wants me."

"Nonsense… I don't believe you!"

"Well… I don't care if you don't believe me." Sally pleaded, her face screwed up in anger. "…It's true!"

"I'm not listening to any of that…." Pat argued. "… You could start by taking a leaf out your big sisters book and get yourself a job… a proper job… And a man as well!"

"Oh for Christ's sake mother…" Sally shouted. "… I'm sixteen… I've just left school… I've got my whole life in front of me. I don't need a man… and I've no intention of tying the knot with the first one who comes along … especially one like Jerry Thompson!"

"Why…?" Sally's mum protested. "And what's up with Jerry… He's a good man?"

"I'll tell you what he is…" Said Sally. "… He's old…he's fat… and he's ugly!"

Pat Fraser stared at her youngest in dismay.

"You better be quiet girl." She said eventually. "…Or else."

"Or…?" Sally lowered her voice. "…Or else what… what are you going to do… kick me out… is that what dad wants as well?"

"I can't speak for your father." Pat answered a little more subdued. "…He can speak for himself… when he comes back from the pub."

"The pub…?" Sally said defiantly. "Oh… so he's escaped to the pub again has he… well we all need to escape now and again mother… perhaps I'll join him?"

Sally's mum looked even more grim-faced and unsympathetic after the last few comments but still she held it together and waited her moment… and then she spoke.

"He's with Jerry… I've just dropped them off a few minutes ago." She smiled sweetly. "… The Imperial… they're meeting up with a few of your dads old army mates."

"It won't last you know… Susie's marriage." Sally growled.

"Well… it best." Said Pat. "… Because they're having a baby."

"What…?" Screamed Sally. "…Have you gone completely bonkers… what the hell are you talking about?"

"Your sister." Said Pat proudly. "…Susie… she's pregnant… she's having a baby. She invited us over this afternoon, to tell us the good news, and that's why your Dad's gone to the pub with Jerry… they're having a few pints to celebrate."

"Oh yeah…" Said Sally. "So… why was I not invited… am I not important?"

"You had an interview… didn't you… or that's what you told us?"

"Yeah… some interview." Sobbed Sally. "But still… you could have told me!"

"I've just told you… haven't I?" Insisted Pat. "So… what's your problem… because now you know?"

It was often quite lively at the Imperial but on that particular evening the customers were positively raucous. Apart from the regulars there was a darts match in progress against another rival pub. The team members of which had brought with them a large contingent of high-spirited girlfriends and wives, each of them trying hard to compete with yet another noisy crowd of other young women celebrating what appeared to be a colleague's imminent divorce. Add to that Jerry Thompson with a couple of his beefy mates and not forgetting Bob Fraser with his motley crew of ex-servicemen, and the atmosphere was electric.

Stories of Bob's exploits during the Korean war soon became the main topic of conversation and even though he wouldn't contribute a great deal in order to embellish his already notorious reputation, his old mates were determined to do that for him quite willingly.

In 1950 Bob Fraser had been stationed in Hong Kong with the Argyll and Sutherland Highlanders when hostilities started. He was nineteen years old. He was put on a ship that took four days to sail to the Korean peninsula during which time he spent most of his time training to shoot properly. When he arrived he became part of the United Nations force who immediately gave him the opportunity to improve his newly acquired skills and what he soon discovered... was that he was very good at it. He also discovered a country of hills with wild rugged beauty and despite the dangers and deprivations it was somewhere he could make his mark doing something that would inevitably shape his character.

Bob made his first kill with a standard issue Lee Enfield 303 rifle, a popular gun used by the majority of British troops during the first world -war. However many of his subsequent targets were eliminated by an assortment of different weapons. The Chinese would attack in the dead of night, their rapid advances often accompanied by trumpet and bugle blowing to create as much fear as possible through the ranks of the U.N. troops. Bob would lie there in the rat-infested darkness waiting for his moment to pounce and when it came, he would strike quickly and with such ferocity that any retaliation was inconceivable.

The enemy hadn't got a prayer.

Bob Fraser was a natural born killer.

But… after many months of hand-to-hand fighting it was inevitable that Bob's days in Korea were numbered. He was a risk taker and that could mean only one thing… inevitably he would be injured, killed or captured. And that's exactly what happened. A dead British soldier had lay in "No Mans Land" for days on end waiting for someone to try and reclaim the body. The threat from Chinese snipers had prevented anyone from attempting such an undertaking until Bob decided to give it a go. After crawling out across fifty yards of scarred inhospitable terrain he reached his fallen comrade, but immediately the Booby Trapped body exploded and Bob was thrown high up into the air, his lifeless frame smashed against the ground and in all probability he too was dead.

Somehow he was dragged back into the trenches by American troops and airlifted to a Mobile Army Surgical Hospital further South. He never regained consciousness until he was transferred to Japan where he spent many months recovering from his ordeal. Once on the mend however he intended to make sure that his convalescence would be as educational and more importantly as pleasurable as possible. And in the company of other injured soldiers, mainly Americans, it was hardly surprising that Bob spent a lot of his recovery time with what the G.I.'s would call "Geesha Girls."

When Bob returned to "Blighty" he was a different man.

It was closing time at the Imperial and as the customers drifted away into the night, Bob made sure that his new son-in-law had secured himself a cab and headed off back to the hills, before he himself began his short walk back to the house.

He staggered along up Union Street past the old Grammar School a beautiful ornate property and now a satellite campus of Preston Polytechnic. During the hot summer it had witnessed a college student sit-in protest, the building occupied on an organized twenty-four hour schedule and even now as Bob trudged by, the ancient exterior was still littered with placards and posters, the old girl hardly recognizable from her early days as a place of exemplary learning.

He pressed on head down incredibly weary, temples throbbing still lost in a haze of wagging tongues, sweaty bodies and mucky beer. Bob sucked in his breath and shuddered as the cold night air brought him to his senses but then suddenly… as he reached St Lawrence's Church across from the Odeon Cinema buildings he saw a tiny figure huddled up on the old stonewall.

Bob screwed up his face and stared into the gloom. The streetlights were poor and he couldn't quite make her out but then eventually as he came closer, he could tell she was young, not as young as his two girls, but not much older and quite a wild rough looking girl. Undoubtedly she was very attractive and even at a distance exuded a raw unsophisticated beauty.

He smiled appraisingly taking in the rigid proud cut of her shoulders, the long blonde hair cascading down the back of her short denim jacket and what he suspected were sharp blue eyes hidden by the shadows. Instantly she acknowledged him and returned his smile, completely unfazed by the approach of a stranger.

"You're that guy aren't you?" She said abruptly. "… The one they were all talking about in the pub."

"Sorry… I didn't catch you?" Bob answered tentatively.

"The war hero?" She insisted. "… You're him aren't you?"

Bob hesitated… he wasn't quite sure what to think.

For a long agonizing minute he stared at the girl, his brain still scrambled from all the alcohol and excitement.

"Don't look so shocked…" She smiled again. "… I'm impressed!"

"Well… you needn't be." He replied eventually. "…It was all a long time ago."

"Did you get a medal…?" She asked.

"Oh… yeah… we all got a medal." Bob laughed. "…Loads of them."

"Really…?" She grinned.

"Yeah really… its no big deal. You get a medal just for turning up."

"No you don't." She giggled.

"Yeah… trust me." Said Bob. "They're called campaign medals."

"But you've got others as well… haven't you." She demanded to know. "… I heard them all talking about it. "

She patted the top of the wall gently and gave him a big smile suspecting he might not want to say any more. She could tell from the look on his face he was reluctant to talk about it any further but nevertheless still encouraged him to sit down beside her.

"The thing is…" Said Bob as he slumped down on the hard stone surface. "Once someone knows something about you… they can't leave you alone… its human nature. They see you as some sort of oddity. I'm not like other people and they can't understand it. First of all they get interested and then the more they learn about you, the more suspicious they become. In the end it all goes pear-shaped. Trust me, I know what I'm talking about."

"Don't tell me then… " She insisted. "… I don't want to know… not about the war anyway."

"Good…" Said Bob. "… Have you got a cigarette?"

"I haven't." Said the girl. "… I wish I had."

"Well not to worry." Bob sighed. "…Because I've got one in my pocket, so if you want to share it… we can do… its up to you?"

"Are you sure…?" Said Blondie.

"Yeah… sure."

They sat for a while chatting about all sorts of things, anything that is apart from Bob's murky past and because he was unwilling to talk about himself, he couldn't very well question her about times gone by. The only thing she did offer was that her scumbag boyfriend had dropped her, yet again, and this time there was no going back.

"Well don't worry… its his loss…." Bob insisted. "…He's a loser…you're a pretty lass… there's a lot of guys out there would bend over backwards to have a girl like you on their arm."

"Would you…?" She said looking him straight in the eye.

"Me…I'm too old…?" Bob grinned. "…But then again… if I was twenty years younger?"

She kissed him immediately on the check… then burst out laughing. "So what do you think about that then?" She asked.

"I think it's probably best if I head off." Said Bob as he slid his bottom off the wall and got to his feet.

"Are you sure…?" The girl reached out and grabbed Bob's jacket pulling him back towards her. She threw her arms tight around his neck angled her face and forced her mouth against his… willing him to respond. In those first few seconds Bob could have and most certainly should have pushed her away and walked on… but he didn't…. and the longer it lasted, the more he wanted it to continue. It was a long frantic kiss and when it finished, they just stared at each other, eager to continue but uncertain of what might follow.

Then suddenly she made a move and touched him between the legs, moving her hand slowly, caressing him, the soft pressure of her fingers like nothing he'd experienced for a very long time. But then almost as quickly as if she'd changed her mind, she stopped what she was doing, and grabbed his hand instead.

"Come on… follow me." The girl whispered. "I know somewhere…"

In less than a minute they were beyond the reach of prying eyes hidden away in the shadows behind Saint Lawrence's Church but struggling hopelessly. It was some distance from the road and a lot darker there and as the girl stumbled over in the churchyard Bob reached out to steady her and as he did so, they both fell forwards astride a huge stone slab. An ancient tomb with a flat horizontal surface covered in moss and lichen standing no more than two feet off the ground… the girl landing clumsily on top of him.

Undeterred they kissed and again she touched him on the side of his face and guided his hand where previously it hadn't dared to go. And when she opened her legs for him and he touched what could be his… he was never going to refuse her.

Bob slipped his free hand down to his belt unbuckling it in a flash and in the same movement dragged his pants down over his thighs.

She squirmed and wriggled above him trying to free herself from the skimpy white knickers or that's what it looked like. Bob realizing instantly that she was more generous than what he had at first thought, though to him that was no bad thing, and so he helped her pull them off and cast them to one side.

And then finally unimpeded… she slid down onto him slowly and as he entered her… she gasped loudly… crying with delight.

When it was all over they got to their feet quickly and began to dress, Bob fumbling nervously with his trousers, the girl picking up her panties and stuffing them straight into her pocket. He turned to face her, she looked disheveled, but then again so did he, and then strangely she just stood arms by her side staring at him intently. It was if she waiting for him to hold her once more and say something kind and reassuring, but he didn't know what to do or what to say… so he said… and did… nothing.

"I know you… don't I?" She said suddenly a slight harshness in her voice.

She's Missing

Bob didn't answer.

"You're Sally Fraser's dad... aren't you?" The girl insisted.

Bob gasped... if the old tomb could have opened up at that very moment and swallowed him completely he would have been grateful. But it didn't.

"You should have said." Bob growled.

"Why...does it matter...?' She asked softly. "Does it really make any difference?"

"Hell yeah...!" Snapped Bob as he zipped up his jacket. "... Bloody right it does."

"Well... I don't care." The girl was insistent. "...And neither should you." She grabbed his hand. "And by the way... my names Maggie... Maggie Sutcliffe... and Bob... I want to see you again... okay?"

Bob didn't answer... he was too busy thinking.

" Come on..." She smiled. " ... You must have guessed by now... I'm a bad lot... I know... I can't deny it. So... will you see me?"

"Yeah okay..." Bob agreed... a slight hint of inevitability in his voice. "We'll meet again..."

"When...?' Said Maggie.

"Soon..." Bob whispered. "...Soon... I promise."

K. E. Heaton

Chapter 7

It was half day closing in Chorley on a Wednesday afternoon. Susie had remained in the office with a few members of staff allowing Jerry to go back to the cottage in White Coppice to begin work on what they both affectionately called the "babies room." It was still quite early in Susie's pregnancy, but Jerry just couldn't wait and if he started now and did a little bit each week, everything would be ready in plenty of time.

It was a lovely south facing room that he reckoned would be a joy to decorate, full of warm light all day long. They'd decided on a soft pavilion blue that Susie had insisted would create a wonderful watery seaside look with bright white woodwork to match, perfect for their first child and hopefully the first of many.

He hadn't been there long and hardly begun when he heard someone knocking on the window downstairs. Reluctantly he stopped work, downed tools and made his way to the front door. When he got there and pulled the door open he was more than surprised, if there was one person he hadn't expected… it was Sally!

"Hey… Jerry." She grinned. "So… how are things with you?"

"I'm okay Sal…" He answered tentatively. "And tell me… what are you doing here?"

One look at Sally and it wasn't hard to see she'd been exercising. She had a face that was positively crimson, a pale grey t-shirt soaked in sweat, straggly locks of wet hair hanging down in front of her sweet little face and a captivating smile that could snare the pope.

"Just out running that's all…" Sally's mouth had gone dry. "… And then I thought to myself why not… let's go visit my big sister… see what she's up to?"

"You've run from Chorley?" He asked.

"Yeah…" She laughed. "Its not that far… not when you're fit."

"Okay…I get it" Jerry patted his large beer belly very gently and sneered. "Point taken…. unfortunately though… you're out of luck Sal… she's back at the office."

"Oh… that's a shame." Said Sally trying her best to sound convincing. "… So what are you doing here Jerry… all on your own?"

"The babies room…" He said proudly. "…It's got to be right."

"Can I look…?" She asked.

"Nothing to see yet." He insisted. "I've hardly started.

"I could do with a drink?"

Jerry sighed. "You better come in then…" He didn't want to stop work but what else could he do? "…There's juice in the fridge Sal…" He added. "But other than that… your only other option is regular corporation pop."

"Yeah…that's fine." Sal agreed. "…Thanks Jerry."

Jerry was well aware of the unhealthy relationship between his new wife and her younger sister, Susie told him everything. It was a shame. The girls had a lot in common. The siblings were both independent, intelligent, pretty young women and the sight of Sally leaning against the kitchen sink in only a pair of tiny shorts and a skimpy t-shirt made him realize how much alike they really were… in particular their physical appearance.

Sal's hair was much shorter than Susie's but exactly the same color. She had a tiny face and a long elegant neck that gave her a rare impish quality, mischievous and naughty. Her legs were strong and athletic certainly more defined than Susie's but still very pleasing to the eye.

And the hourglass figure that Susie had been blessed with was more than evident in her little sister.

Sally stretched out to prevent herself from stiffening up and the more she stretched the more athletic and leggy she appeared. Her actions however negligible had not gone unnoticed. Jerry moved a little closer sidling over towards her very slowly and then finally as Sally turned to face him, he whispered in her ear.

"The thing is Sal… I need to get some work done." He insisted. "… You understand?"

"Yeah… okay." She said abruptly. "I get it… you don't want me here."

"That's not what I said…"

"No… you're probably right." Said Sal suddenly. "… I need to get going anyway… can I use your bathroom?"

"Of course." Jerry answered despairingly. "…Of course you can… up the stairs… second on the left."

Sally disappeared. He didn't trust her one bit, but could hardly follow her, it didn't seem right. He had a feeling she was up to go good but in danger of over-reacting he stayed well out of her way. If he paid her too much attention he might be misunderstood and so he let her get on with whatever it was she needed to do… hopefully all she actually wanted was a pee.

In truth Sally Fraser had other things on her mind and it wasn't building bridges. She'd heard her mum talking to Susie that morning on the telephone and when she learned that Jerry was going to be home alone that afternoon Sal decided there and then to put her plan into action. As far as she was concerned anything that was good enough for Susie was good enough for her and the one thing Susie treasured more than anything else, she could also take away.

Jerry waited and he waited and waited but still Sal didn't reappear. The least he'd expected was the sound of the toilet flushing or a creak on the stairs to say she was on her way back down… but nothing. Eventually… devoid of any other great ideas he decided to shout her and see if she might respond.

"Sal…" Jerry growled. "… Are you okay up there?"

Still nothing.

"Sally…!" He tried again. "… Are you alright… for god's sake?"

Jerry walked along the hallway and began slowly tentatively to climb the stairs… what else could he do? In the absence of any other sound in the house the arrival of every footstep seemed incredibly noisy, the stairs excessively creaky, each gasp of Jerry's breathe magnified a hundred times. He tiptoed up step by step until he reached the top, pausing for a split second before moving on very gradually towards the bathroom door. He hesitated, listened then rapped the center of the door with the back of his knuckles, when he failed to get a reply he turned the door handle and pushed the door wide open. The room was empty. Jerry crept along the landing until he got to the main bedroom door. And… when finally he reached it, found it wasn't completely closed. The edge of the door was literally millimeters away from its old discolored framework allowing a tiny chink of light to escape onto the landing.

"Sal…?" He whispered. "…Are you in there?"

Jerry waited five, six, seven seconds maybe until finally he pushed the door open very, very gently... and what he revealed was totally bizarre. Sally was lying on the big double bed completely naked. She was on her right hand side facing away from the door. She'd drawn her left leg up and rested her bent knee on three large pillows positioned one on top of the other on the far side of the bed. She was slim and lithe and with her clothes off appeared much smaller, her shape well proportioned, her skin smooth completely unblemished. She had a lovely white bottom that glistened with sweat a stark contrast between the dark skin of her thighs and lower back. Jerry didn't speak he just watched her smoothing her hair back when suddenly Sal's hand disappeared between her legs.

He was so close to her he could hear her breathing. Almost immediately her hips began to move in a very particular way and he could hear the faintest of sounds emanating from her lips. It came from deep inside her a grateful sound of self-indulgence and untamed pleasure. He was tempted to scream at her and demand that she get the fuck off his bed immediately but there was something very basic, very primeval about what she was doing and therefore Jerry hesitated... loath to disturb such intimacy... reluctant to spoil the fun.

Sally Fraser was positively feral.

"Are you enjoying this Jerry...?" She whispered suddenly. "...Are you?"

Jerry didn't answer... he didn't need to... she already knew.

Sally rolled over to face him and giggled loudly… her body moving gently in rhythm with her hand. And still… Jerry didn't speak he just stood there fascinated by her actions absorbed in the whole experience and desperate for more. She slid to the edge of the bed very slowly allowing her legs to fall to the floor before finally she stood upright and placed a hand on either hip.

"How would you like me Jerry…? " She asked sweetly. "We can do anything you want… anything at all… just say!"

He stepped forward and kissed her on the mouth and then her small breasts as she gripped his upper arms tightly and pressed down onto them as hard as she could until eventually he got the hint and dropped to his knees. Then… resting her palm on the top of his head she forced him down even further until his head was now between her legs and immediately he pushed his mouth against her. She shivered briefly and moved away but then just as quickly pushed herself towards him yet again and allowed him to lick her furiously.

She ruffled his hair vigorously twisting each strand around her fingers pulling his head backwards and forwards as he continued to excite her. Until eventually she struggled free and fell back on the bed laughing loudly at the top of her voice watching Jerry fumbling with his trousers as he tried to drag them off. And then finally when he was free diving onto her pulling himself up until his head was once again between her thighs, Sal opening her legs as wide as she possibly could… daring him to devour her. But then screaming frantically when she realized that Jerry had accepted the challenge and had pinned her to the bed with his big strong arms, each of her thighs held tightly in a vice like grip, his tongue wriggling furiously inside her, her genitalia all juiced up, pink and swollen and flushed with color.

She punched him in the head and dragged her fingernails over his back time and time again but still he wouldn't relent until almost at a point when she thought she might just feint… suddenly… he released his grip… pulled himself up gradually until his body was aligned with hers then penetrated her completely.

When Sally arrived back home in Chorley late afternoon she was utterly exhausted. She'd done exactly what she intended and more importantly she'd got away with it. And as the hot shower washed all over her and took away all the torrid smells of debauchery and made her clean again she believed that she Sally Fraser was in control… of everything… and everybody.

Nobody could touch her… nobody… how little did she know?

Chapter 8

Only September but already the nights were drawing in fast. It was a chilly night in Lancashire with a grey over-cast sky and a beastly wind and so the two walked quickly, heads down, away from prying eyes and into the shadows.

The prospect of a stroll through Astley Park could be quite daunting at night especially alone but at dusk when the light was fading fast and strange shapes appeared out of nowhere as if by magic, it was not a place for the feint hearted. Huge trees still laden with summer leaves swayed from side to side in the distance like drunken giants but seemingly even more threatening and nearer to the path were masses of rhododendron wild and unruly. Guardians of the wood on either side, ground troops with long straggly arms ready to snare you if you dared to come any closer.

Pat Fraser however was no shrinking violet and neither was her companion. They'd done this walk many times before on numerous occasions and especially in the dark when others couldn't see them and what they didn't see… they couldn't blab about.

When Pat left home a little earlier the house was silent. Bob had gone back to the pub… or so he said and that was fine with her. And Sally after yet another grueling run… or so she said… had collapsed on the sofa and gone straight to sleep.

Inexplicably for a girl of Sal's age she appeared completely exhausted. And that made Pat wonder a little but it was convenient and meant that Pat didn't have to explain herself as she so often did and fabricate some new story about where she was going and what she was doing.

Her and Billy Marsden went back a long time.

Somehow she'd managed to stay in touch and see him on a regular basis for almost twenty years and never once in that huge expanse of time had she ever uttered his name to another living sole.

She loved Billy and she always would. He was her first love and as far as men go… her only love. He was married with two kids exactly like Pat and lived in the village of Eccleston about six miles from the center of Chorley.

When Pat needed to confide in someone and when she needed a friend, a proper friend, Billy was always there to give her moral support. It was the only thing he had been able to give her but to Pat it was a lifeline and a shoulder to cry on when things got tough. Like her… his family ties were also complicated and if the truth ever came out it wouldn't do anyone any good, it would shatter so many lives and upset so many people, it wasn't an option.

Billy was a tall smart handsome man with short clipped mahogany colored hair and an honest face. On the wrong side of forty he had seen better days but if Pat could exchange him for the cruel drunken scumbag that she'd been forced to marry, she'd do it in an instant.

As the daughter of a Presbyterian minister with staunch protestant roots Pat was indoctrinated with stories of John Calvin who escaped the persecution of catholic France and headed for Geneva and then subsequently the free city of Strasbourg. Whereas Billy Marsden was on the opposite side of a huge divide and part of a strong Roman Catholic family that would never tolerate even the thought of one of their own changing their allegiance. And so… when Pat got pregnant any chance of marriage to Billy was out of the question.

Within days of finding out Pat had found herself a new man. She slept with Bob Fraser on the very first date and a few weeks later declared her condition. As far as Bob Fraser knew… Susie was his, but what he could never know was that actually… her real dad was Billy.

As far as Pats family were concerned Bob Fraser was an ideal partner for their daughter. A white Anglo Saxon protestant male who'd served queen and country and had returned from Korea a recognized war hero. When they met him for the first time he was still in uniform, his chest littered with medals. He seemed friendly enough and even though he was not the most talkative of men he appeared very respectful especially to his new in-laws and when he asked for Pats hand in marriage, it was a forgone conclusion.

The reality however was something completely different. Pat realized very quickly that Bob was a violent abusive man who when questioned could loose his temper in seconds. He hit her several times even before Susie was born but it was after that when things soon escalated out of control.

And then… a few weeks before Susie's second birthday Bob came home one night from the pub in an angry mood. He demanded sex and Pat refused him. He dragged her to the floor and kicked her repeatedly. Tore every inch of clothing from her body and threw her on the bed. He raped her savagely and during this attack she suffered a concussion, a broken nose and a dislocated thumb in her vain attempt to fight him off and despite a call to the police from worried neighbors, the authorities did nothing. Bob was a war hero who'd left the UK shores and risked life and limb defending democracy against a growing worldwide communist threat and for that they cut him some slack. Okay he'd returned home with a few problems, nothing too serious and what he needed now was some respect and admiration and a little time to readjust. The whole sordid event was swept under the carpet and considered a private matter between husband and wife. And as the police described it… "It was just a domestic."

Thirty-five weeks later Sally arrived into the world bawling and screaming exactly like her father. She'd inherited his good looks but on the down side all his peculiar mannerisms and his violent temper.

It was hardly any wonder that Pat considered Susie her special child and the one most beautiful gift she had ever received from God. But as for Sally… she was the devil itself, conceived in an orgy of lust and violence and a constant reminder of how much she hated the man she'd married.

"So…" Said Billy as they sat down in the shelter. "… Our little girl… suddenly she's wed and now she's having a baby?"

"She is…" Said Pat excitedly. "…Its good news…its happy news… I'm pleased for them… honestly I am."

"I wish I could have been the one to walk her up the aisle." Said Billy with some regret.

"Me too Bill." Pat agreed.

"And is he a kind man… Jerry?" Asked Bill sounding more than a little concerned.

"I believe so…" Said Pat. "I've no reason to think otherwise… and I've never heard anyone speak a bad word about him… the main thing is Susie seems very contented."

"That's good…" Insisted Billy. "I'm glad… she deserves to be happy… she's a good girl."

It was about six thirty by the time Susie got home. A couple of late phone calls into the office delayed her departure, a bit of a nuisance but in Jerry's absence she had no option but to take them, something she may not have done a few weeks previous. But now that she was the boss's wife she felt obliged to set a good example.

It gave Jerry a valuable amount of additional time to get the house sorted out and God knows he needed it. Sally looked all done in when she left the house but at least she'd left quietly and immediately he sprang into action. He was determined to cover his tracks and make sure that Susie never found out about what had happened that day. When she got back the house would have to be exactly as it should be with no hint that Sally had ever been there. He'd already made up his mind that if Sal ever tried to use it against him, he'd call her bluff. After all, everyone knew that she was the biggest troublemaker ever, a devious mischief and a compulsive liar. And therefore, he had to ensure that everything was in order with no clue, indicator or any evidence whatsoever that might substantiate the credibility of anything Sally might say in the future. Anything she did say Jerry would dismiss as simply a malicious, wicked and ridiculous accusation.

He started by racing around the house opening every single window as wide as possible then made his way back to the main bedroom to clean up. The quilt cover was horribly wet and sticky, hardly surprising really after such a heavy session but a stark reminder of what had happened. Since the wedding he'd made love to Susie several times on that very same bed but what he'd experienced with Susie bore no resemblance to events that afternoon.

What he and Sally had just done was nothing short of dirty, erotic and downright disgusting. He hated himself for joining in but still he couldn't escape the amazing image of that filthy bitch lying on his bed with her legs wide open screaming for more.

He changed the duvet cover and the pillows and hurried downstairs with the soiled items, stripped off completely and threw all his clothes and the bedding into the same wash. He searched the house frantically for anything else that might incriminate him then ran back up to the baby's room. He slapped a bit more paint on here and there then purposely left the lid of the paint can slightly open allowing the fumes to waft in and around the bedrooms. He took the brushes down to the utility room and left them soaking in a large tin filled with turpentine. As an after thought he grabbed one of the rags he'd used to wipe them with and ran upstairs yet again and left it on the window sill in the main bedroom. It was temporary measure until Susie came home but it was something Jerry was convinced would mask the lingering smell of Susie's sweaty body and anything else that had happened in there.

It was a distinct odor that permeated not only that room but in addition the whole of the upstairs living space. Then finally he jumped in the shower and proceeded to scrub himself clean taking great care to rid himself of even the slightest hint of indiscretion.

A few minutes later he was dried and dressed again in a clean shirt and trousers and as far as Jerry was concerned he was squeaky clean.

When he saw Susie's mini pull up outside he opened the door to greet her gave her a big kiss on the cheek and helped her with her stuff.

"God Jerry…" Exclaimed Susie immediately. "… What on earth is that smell?"

"Oh yeah..." Said Jerry casually. "... I'm sorry about that... We've had a bit of an accident."

"Yeah okay..." Insisted Susie. "... But what is it?"

"Its probably turpentine that you can smell.... is it that noticeable?'

"Noticeable?" She repeated. "...Its horrible."

Susie stepped inside proper her eyes acutely alert to what was going on.

"Why turpentine Jerry?' She asked. "Its awful... I can't believe you can't smell it... what happened?"

"Okay... I'll tell you." He said reluctantly. "I'm an idiot... I know. I started the painting without getting changed first and then suddenly when I realised I had some gloss on my trousers I dashed in the bedroom to get changed but unfortunately I still had the paint brush in my hand. And what did I do next...? I dropped it... on the quilt."

"Oh... you're messing Jerry." Susie gasped.

"No... I'm afraid not." He admitted. "But listen... it's all sorted now... everything's in the wash... there's nothing to worry about... okay?"

"Yeah, yeah okay." She agreed. "But turpentine... surely there must be something else you could have used?"

"I've opened all the windows."

"Alright…" She acknowledged. "But I suggest you open all the doors as well… it stinks in here…. and if you think I'm cooking…?"

"No… no don't worry." Jerry interjected. "We'll go to the Yew Tree tonight… Its my treat."

Susie went upstairs alone and got changed. She was sure that he wouldn't want her to look in the baby's room to see what he'd already accomplished but she had a peek anyway and wondered immediately why after all this time… he'd barely made a start.

Susie had clopped up and downstairs from her comfortable snug living room to her lovely bedroom many, many times since Jerry had purchased the cottage, and every step was familiar. Susie knew every grain of the floorboards and every ruck in the carpet and now she was so acquainted with the old place she doubted very much if she could ever live anywhere else. But since she'd left the house to go to work that morning there had been subtle almost unnoticeable changes but as Susie had registered… they were changes nevertheless.

Chapter 9

About ten o' clock the following morning Sally predictably was still at home. She'd slept like a log and only woke when Pat shouted her. It was a daily routine... her Dad left for work and then her Mum... but it was her Mum who complained bitterly when Sally wasn't up before she left the house. Pat didn't see why they should be up every morning bright and early and allow their youngest to lie in with no prospect of a job on the horizon and from what she could determine Sally's total lack of motivation to do anything else apart from taking her daily run and then subsequently raiding the fridge on her return.

Sally did however move pretty sharpish when someone knocked really hard three times on the front door. She peered through the lounge window to see who it was and recognized the regular postman immediately.

"Sally Fraser... it must be your birthday?" He smiled handing her a strange looking parcel.

"No... I don't think so." She snapped. "... But thanks."

Sally had seen a parcel wrapped just like this before... it was exactly like Susie had brought home from the office all those weeks ago... the one from Tom Smith... returning her sisters shoes after her night on the moors. This too was a large mysterious package securely wrapped in shiny brown paper and all tied up with a huge length of string.

She closed the door behind her ambled her way back along the hallway and sat down at the bottom of the stairs hesitated for a moment then began slowly to unfasten the parcel very, very carefully.

What she found was quite bizarre.

There were two separate articles of clothing, a tiny white envelope containing a single piece of paper folded once down the center, a twenty-pound note and what looked like a black jewelers box about six inches long and two inches wide, its lid embossed in simple modest gold lettering identifying its famous manufacturer "Pierre C. Cartier."

She fingered the outfit as it laid across her lap a sheer black silk chiffon top with red polka dots, ruffled sleeves and a long black satin tie. It had with it a black cotton velvet skirt simply cut at the hips but which released into a full circle at about knee height with a flared hem. It was flirty and raunchy and Sal loved it immediately. She searched frantically for a label knowing all too well that this was no off the peg skirt from the local rag trade. And then suddenly she found what she was looking for in fact she found two. The first one said simply "Made in France" the second "Yves Saint Laurent."

Sally got to her feet and slipped the skirt over her knickers… it was perfect, the chiffon top also, in fact both of the items were truly exquisite.

She sat down again quickly to read the note and considering that she already had a previous one addressed to her sister, a letter that Susie had never seen, Sal had a pretty good idea already of what it might say.

The letter began…

"Hello Sal,

I'm very upset that last time we met you left in such a hurry and we didn't say goodbye.

I was an idiot and I'm really sorry. I just couldn't handle it when you thought that I was sleeping around. Despite what people say about me I'm not such a bad guy. I'm just like everyone else out there looking for someone special.

I think I've found her that special person but I've messed up big time and now I might never get her back.

So, if you come over on Saturday around 7.00pm I'll prove to you that I can be trusted and I promise to treat you like a lady and look after you.

And if you do come we can be together just you and I. We have a lovely big house here, somewhere you could be happy and I'm sure that its somewhere you could make your home. It's where you belong.

Tom.

PS.- I hope you like the frock, it's for you to wear on our special date. Please find also enclosed a twenty-pound note to pay for your taxi and a little bit of something extra a special gift from me to you."

Sally was flattered by Tom's comments and impressed with his choice of outfit, but Sal knew all too well what effect she could have on the opposite sex… and so… even though she was delighted with what he'd given her… she was not surprised.

The question was… would she go?

It was hard to decide… very hard, until she opened the "Cartier" box… and then… well by then it was probably a forgone conclusion.

Inside the box were two lovely and very heavy items of fine jewelry. Both pieces made from eighteen-karat gold and each decorated with numerous brilliantly cut diamonds. A sparkly necklace and matching bracelet each of them stamped with the "Cartier" name and then "Italy 18K" and then subsequently their individual serial numbers.

What Tom Smith had undoubtedly given her was a gift way beyond her expectations and something that she realized was worth an absolute fortune.

If Tom Smith could give her this now before she'd even agreed to meet him, what could he offer her if one day she decided to married him?

Sal was under no illusions the guy was complex and hard to understand but if he had access to such great wealth he could give her literally anything she wanted. But not only that, now she had the overwhelming ability to diminish and belittle her big sister and everything she'd done in recent months. Already she'd managed to seduce Susie's husband and with Tom Smith by her side with his power and his money she could achieve almost anything… anything at all.

Would she go to Tom Smith's house on Saturday? … There was nothing, absolutely nothing that could keep her away!

"You alright Susan…?"

Susie nodded although her eyes stayed focused on the house. They were sitting in Jerry's car outside the cottage ready to drive into the office, but at the last minute she decided to leave him to it.

"No…" She said suddenly. "I'm not alright… I'm feeling sick… you know what, you carry on… I'll follow you in later!"

Susie allowed him to kiss her gently on the cheek then got out of the car and went back inside. Jerry waited for a short while just in case she changed her mind but then eventually he drove off, hoping that's all it was. Susie feeling sick was one thing but his recent indiscretion was something else.

She lifted the curtain and watched him go wondering if any of the neighbors, few as they were, had any idea who lived here. Surely she thought they must notice who comes and goes, but even if they did, they kept themselves to themselves. So much for people being friendlier in the country. If this were the center of Chorley the neighbors would know everything.

And then suddenly she realized that there was something about Jerry that irritated her. Maybe it was the way in which he combed his hair, his aftershave or the pathetic need to rattle his heavy gold signet bracelet as he walked around the house. She couldn't be sure but whatever it was she hadn't noticed any of those annoying peculiarities a few weeks ago but now the more she thought about it… it was perhaps all those things.

She made her way to the bathroom convinced that this time she was definitely about to throw up but as usual once she'd sat down on the loo for a few minutes the nausea soon disappeared and she wondered whether she'd made a big fuss about nothing.

And thankfully a day later, the bathroom didn't smell so much of paint and turpentine, the bedroom either, as she walked back in there to grab her cardigan.

Susie stared at the bed somewhat suspiciously and immediately she noticed something out of place. She knelt on the floor and stretched her right arm underneath the bed until her shoulder was wedged against the frame proceeding to run her hand across the carpet. The bed had been expensive but looked a little small now for a double. She doubted very much in a few months if it would take the weight of a big guy like Jerry and a heavily pregnant woman.

And as she moved her arm from side to side sweeping the underside it was then her hand brushed against it for the first time. She repeated the exercise until eventually she managed to grasp it between her fingers and pull it out from the side of the bed. It was such a simple little thing but nevertheless as Susie realized straight away of great significance. A tiny fluorescent green hair bobble that she knew immediately was not hers.

"Surely not…!" Susie whispered to herself.

She shook her head in disbelief stepped across to the dresser and picked up a photograph of her and Jerry outside the church running towards the camera, huge smiles on their faces.

Susie squeezed her eyes shut and without realizing dug her nails into the side of the photo frame but then almost immediately released her grip, opening her eyes just in time to see it crash to the floor, its glass disintegrating into what appeared to be thousands of sharp tiny splinters.

Susie chose to leave the house and go for a long walk and only then would she be able to decide what to do. What she now recognized as Sally's unmistakable odor and recent presence in the cottage disturbed her. She exited the gate at the top of the cricket field and began her walk along the footpath at the side of the "Goit." An old watercourse used for transporting drinking water along the Rivington reservoir chain, a path that if she wished to follow would take her all the way from White Coppice to the village of Brinscall almost two miles away. And so she strode on head down oblivious to anything around her. Her eyes were glassy her face flushed.

She wanted to scream but when she opened her mouth no words came out. Susie's daily nausea may have subsided but another much greater sickening feeling had replaced it… it was a feeling of bitter betrayal that welled up inside her stomach.

She reached Brinscall in less than thirty minutes completely preoccupied with her thoughts.

The truth is she was in shock and never before in her life had she ever felt such excruciating pain, anger and humiliation.

Someone she swore… someone would pay for this.

Chapter 10

It was three in the afternoon before Jerry got through to his wife on the telephone.

"Susie...!" He said calmly. "...I've been worried about you... are you okay?"

"I'm alright..." She answered quietly. "I've been for a walk this morning... and then for a sleep... but I'm not coming in."

"No...it doesn't matter." He said reassuringly. "I understand... I wasn't ringing for that... I just wanted to know that you were okay."

"Yeah... I'm fine." She said again. "...Are you busy?"

"We're snowed under." He insisted. "It's been manic... Angie has only just gone for her lunch a few minutes ago... but it's all under control."

"So... let me guess." She said. "You're going to be late?"

"Yeah... I'm afraid so." Sighed Jerry. "But if I stay on for a while after closing I can soon get straight again... no problem."

"Do you want me to cook?" Susie asked.

"I was going to suggest I call in at the "Chippy" on the way home... what do you think?"

"Yeah..." Susie agreed. "That's probably a good idea..."

"Okay." He said. I'll ring you just before I leave... see you later... love you."

"Yeah..." Susie's voice tailed off into the distance "... I'll see you later."

Immediately as Jerry replaced the handset he got to his feet stepped across to the office door and closed it securely, sat himself down again and proceeded to make another call. The girls in the office would always try to listen in... and often successfully... but not this time. Jerry's voice was hushed... his body language unusually subdued his demeanor very calm and stoical. He didn't mind who might have listened in to his earlier call, but apart from the person he'd just contacted... he wasn't prepared to share this conversation with anyone.

Jerry ended the call abruptly. His eyes narrowed and he leaned back in the chair, took a deep breath and studied the gold bracelet on his wrist as if it was the first time he'd seen it. He had a lot on his mind and a lot to loose if things went awry. He'd always been a bit of a gambler but the stakes were high. He was noticeably less talkative than usual and a little earlier when one of the ladies asked about Susie he'd deflected the question and suggested they should all get back to work. He considered buying flowers on the way home but mindful that it might send the wrong message and look overly suspicious.

Jerry wandered into the main office and shook his head is dismay.

One of the staff sat hunched over the typewriter muttering away, her hair all tousled from the constant raking with her fingers. Another seemed oblivious to his presence and continued to flick through pages and pages of a recent September edition of Vogue magazine identifying all the clothes that make Britain great, but before she could finish the article and move on to yet another item entitled lots of make-up by Mary Quant, Jerry's voice reverberated around the office demanding attention.

"Right…!" He shouted. "Enough is enough… if I don't get some bloody work out of you lot before six o' clock… then don't bother to come back in the morning… You can all go down to the Labor Exchange… and get yourselves a new job!"

Miraculously the typewriter sprang into action, the photocopier raced backwards and forwards spewing out endless sheets of A4 paper and the Vogue magazine ended up in the bin. And if it wasn't for yet another incoming call on Jerry's telephone his rant would have continued, the boss disappeared once more behind closed doors and before too long the office was back to normal.

His next conversation lasted a lot longer but then finally when the call ended Jerry stared out once more through the glass partition wall that separated his domain from the main office. He sat with his elbows on the desk his head cradled in the framework that his hands and particularly his thumbs provided. Most of his face was concealed behind his fingers although his eyes could still peer out above them and watch the girls as they dashed around the office, still agitated by Jerry's recent remarks.

He was a man who not only adored women but understood them as well and consequently he understood their wrath.

Jerry knew all too well what they were capable of and that was why above all else he feared them.

When he was drunk Bob Fraser said all sorts of crazy things but what you couldn't do was ask him too many questions especially if he'd had as many drinks as he obviously had that afternoon. He was on what they appropriately called staggered shifts and that week he'd started work at six in the morning and finished every afternoon at two o' clock which meant that if he wanted to spend the rest of the day in the pub no one apart from the landlord and a few others boozers was any the wiser. Not until he arrived home of course when he would wander in and make a nuisance of himself at which point Pat and often Sally as well these days would make themselves scarce until he disappeared upstairs and went to bed. On this particular day though, he'd been in Yates Wine Lodge almost four hours and drinking heavily. He was very vocal and by the sounds of it had some sort of axe to grind. Suggesting what given half the chance he'd love to do to someone who'd been disrespectful to him. Some of his mates were tempted to ask whom it was he was talking about but the man was so unpredictable and if he took a dislike to you or he thought you were probing too deeply, he could lash out without warning. As far as Bob Fraser was concerned old habits died hard. By half past six all his buddies had deserted him and he'd decided finally that it was probably time to leave and so he downed his last mouthful of ale and stepped out into the street bleary eyed and considerably worse for wear.

He stumbled along up Market Street towards the town hall in the direction of home when about fifty yards away from "Gladrights" on the opposite side of the road he observed a small familiar female figure waiting in the doorway. It was only for a second maybe two but long enough to identify her without a shadow of a doubt. She was wearing the plainest of dresses with a long wooly cardigan over the top, her hands pushed down in pockets on either side. Her hair was pulled right back and tucked in under a scarf but a few stray wisps of blonde hair had escaped and fluttered in the breeze. She looked nervous and impatient but full of energy and when suddenly he noticed her and saw once again her bare legs… pale and sturdy… he shuddered. Bob hesitated for a moment and watched as the estate agents door opened and in she stepped but then just as quickly it shut behind her and in the blink of an eye she was gone from view.

"Hello Maggie…" Said Jerry calmly. "…It's been a while."

"It has… you're right." Maggie smiled sweetly. "…Have you missed me?"

"What do you think…of course I have?" Jerry answered as he stepped even closer.

"You're a liar Jerry Thompson…" She insisted. "And you know it."

"I've been busy…"

"Busy moving house…" She growled. "And busy getting married…. Or have you forgotten that already?"

Jerry reached out to touch her but she brushed him aside and walked off towards his office. He didn't try to stop her, just the opposite, and instead checked the front door for a second time just to make sure that he'd locked it properly. He gazed down the street in both directions surveying the footpaths on either side and as far as he could determine she hadn't been followed and no one was paying the slightest attention to any of his property features in the window. He took a while longer to be absolutely certain but then finally, satisfied with his surveillance, he followed the girl into his office.

When he walked in Maggie said nothing.

She'd sat down at his desk and laid her face on her arms.

As he approached she swung around suddenly, pushed back the chair and dropped to her knees. She clung on to Jerry's legs still speechless and sobbing.

He lifted her up and held her in his arms.

"I didn't want you to… to get married!" She cried. "That was never your intention… was it?"

Maggie was trying to pretend that he loved her as much as she loved him but the truth was Jerry didn't love anyone… but himself.

"I don't know…" He insisted. "It just happened."

"But why?" Maggie screamed. "Why… do you love her…I thought you and I would…?" But the words died away before she could finish. She was visibly shaken, her body trembling from head to toe and once again she slipped down almost to her knees as Jerry took hold of her by the elbows to lift her up. And as he did so she propelled herself forward into his arms, her full body weight leant against him, her mouth smothering him with kisses. He slid his hands over her hips as she steadied herself in front of him and then slowly his fingers shifted to her waist and she helped him to undress her. He pressed his face against her flesh and breathed in the scent of her warm beautiful skin. Then he kicked off his shoes as she tugged at his trousers until they too were strewn across the floor, tossed aside like everything else and no longer an obstacle to what would follow.

His hands moved up and cupped her breasts they were warm and firm, his fingers circling her nipples, noticeably firmer with every touch. He kissed her neck tenderly then led her to the desk, pushed all the papers and documents to one side then sat down on the edge, rolled onto his back and pulled her towards him, to lie on top of him. And as the office ceiling came into view he entered her. Neither of them spoke. She began immediately to move her body slowly up and down time and time again and he just lay back and stayed hard inside her waiting for her to take control.

And she did exactly that…exactly what he wanted until suddenly her thighs appeared to spasm and twitch as they tightened their grip and she held him even more firmly. It sent shock waves through their bodies and despite her attempt to stay focused she was out of control. The slightest movement produced huge surges of euphoria like she'd never experienced. An intense pleasure that made her scream out loud but at the same time forced her to beg for more. Until eventually Jerry closed his eyes and let go inside her and waited patiently for the madness to subside.

It was eight forty five in the evening when the door to "Gladrights" estate agents opened yet again. A tiny blonde haired girl slipped out on to the street and headed off. She had a raw unsophisticated beauty that men found hard to resist. The sort of girl that men dreamt about and wanted to sleep with and do all sorts of other things with but the sort of girl they were frightened to get involved with. Maggie Sutcliffe was exactly that… the girl that nobody dared to take home.

She was sad and craving attention and desperate to be noticed but what she didn't need was the attention that she was getting from the figure huddled up in the smelly alley on the opposite side of the street known locally as "Peter Wink". Bob Fraser had stood there motionless for over two hours waiting for Maggie to leave the premises and now finally... he had her in his sights.

Chapter 11

Sally was apprehensive about going up to Tom Smith's place on Saturday night but the truth was she couldn't resist. As far as Pat Fraser was aware their youngest daughter was having a sleep over at Anne's house, a lass who Sally had befriended on her first day at school at age five and since then the two girls had remained inseparable. Anne had been a loyal friend to Sally despite the Fraser girl's bad reputation and therefore getting into trouble was nothing new. She helped frequently to antagonize Sally's big sister on lots of occasions and therefore she wasn't one of either Susie's or Pat's favorite guests.

The evening before the big event however Sally did not sleep well, it poured down for most of the night and her bedroom window rattled incessantly. It was yet another repair on the house that Bob Fraser had written down on his "jobs to do" list but like lots of other things that he'd promised to mend, it would never get done.

By mid afternoon Sally had packed all her stuff in the overnight bag including the clothes that Tom had sent her. She didn't want anything to get creased but had no option. If Pat had seen the outfit her youngest daughter was planning to wear that evening up on the West Pennine Moors she'd have locked her up and thrown away the key. What Sal intended however was to spend a few hours at Anne's before she left town during which time she could press the clothes if needed, put her make-up on and then jump in to a taxi all dolled up and ready for action. There was therefore as far as she was concerned nothing that could possibly go wrong but as she made her way down the hallway towards the front door Bob Fraser's loud gravelly voice bellowed after her.

"And where do you think you're off to…?" He snarled.

"I told you the other day." Snapped Sally. "It's a sleep over… at Anne's."

"You never told me." He growled. "So you can forget it… ring her… tell her you're not going."

"What…?" Sal yelled. "Why the hell should I?"

"Because…" He barked angrily. "And don't swear at me Sally Fraser… or else!"

"Or else what…?" Sally screamed. "You'll punch me in the face like you do to everyone who says something you don't like."

Bob Fraser couldn't believe what he was hearing and especially from one of his own. He charged down the hallway after the girl and put himself between her and the door.

"Right then… you cheeky little cow." He sneered menacingly. "Go on… say that again… I dare you."

It was the first time Sal had ever pushed him that far and even though she knew exactly what he was capable of, she'd no intention of backing down. She stared him directly in the eye and repeated her last sentence almost word for word.

"You'll punch me in the face." She whispered. "Just like you do to everyone who says something you don't want to hear... am I right?"

Bob Fraser had never backed down from a confrontation... ever. He believed that if he couldn't get what he wanted by discussion then his fists would do the talking and more than likely they'd do a much better job. He glared at Sal hovering above her, his eyelids flickering, his teeth grinding, he felt a terrible anger coming over him and could feel his finger nails pressing hard into the palms of his hands. His knuckles white and drained of color scarred from previous battles and ready to smash their way through anybody or anything that dared to stand in their path. But then all of a sudden he shook his head from side to side and tried to speak but there was no voice. He'd never experienced anything like it... ever... an overwhelming sensation of physical impotence and for the first time in his life he appeared almost powerless. Instinctively Sal could sense the victory and she'd no intention of backing off, she stared even harder at the man, the man who on countless occasions had beaten her mother, threatened the neighbors and terrorized his so-called buddies. But now suddenly Sal could see right through him... she'd exposed what sort of creature he really was and then gradually... it dawned on her... he couldn't face her any more... unable to meet her steely gaze.

"Get out…" He mumbled suddenly. "Go on… get out… and don't come back. Do you hear me… don't come back?"

Sally brushed past him quickly and ran to the doorway. She grabbed her bag, took one last look at the man whom she'd always considered her nemesis, stepped out onto the path and slammed the door behind her.

As Anne's house came into view Sal's mood lifted. She decided not to dwell on what had just happened but instead concentrated on the night ahead and what sort of goodies that Tom Smith might have to offer. As she approached the property it almost seemed as if she were emerging from a trance. Anne was waiting for her exactly as she'd promised and led the way across the hall and up the stairs to her bedroom. They clambered on to the bed as they always did… young faces flushed with excitement.

"Forgive me." Said Anne reluctantly. "But if I don't say what's on my mind… I'm not being honest with you!"

"Go on…" Said Sal. "Say it… I can probably guess anyway."

"Can you?" Whispered Anne. "…Really?"

"Yeah." Said Sally. "You don't want me to go?"

"How do you know?"

"I can tell." Insisted Sal. "Its not hard."

Anne nodded. She dragged her hand across the eiderdown to make it smooth again then looked up at Sally as she had done on many other previous occasions with those big brown puppy dog eyes.

"He might be dangerous." She gasped.

"Yeah." Said Sal. "You're right he could. But don't forget I've been living with a crazy guy for the past sixteen years and somehow I've managed to survive. If I can handle my old fella then trust me I can manage one solitary night with Tom Smith."

"Your Dad's not crazy." Anne argued. "He's a bad tempered old sod I'll give you that… but he's not crazy."

"What?" Sal growled. "You don't know him… my father's a psychopath… you've got to believe me he's certifiable."

"Well I still don't think you should go to Tom Smith's." Anne tried desperately to convince her. "… I'm begging you Sal…I want you to stay here with me… tonight."

One glimpse of Anne's face revealed what Sally already knew. Anne Turner was obsessed with Sal, she simply adored her, worshipped the very ground she walked on and was undeniably madly in love with her. And it was then the tears came and as she cried Anne started suddenly to produce strange retching sounds, and her whole body began to jerk up and down and Sal could sense the grief inside her, cutting her up, and she knew that with one simple look... after all those years... she'd denied her.

"Please..." Sal insisted. "Listen to me carefully." Sally grabbed her friend's hand and squeezed it firmly. "I know you're concerned but you've just got to trust me. I know what I'm doing and if after this we don't see each other for a while it's because it has to be that way. Do you understand?"

"No not really..." Sobbed Anne. "But obviously you've got something planned."

"Maybe." Said Sal cautiously. "But who knows what the future holds... not me!"

Anne sat back looking puzzled. She would do anything for Sally, literally anything at all... but this time... this time it was different, she didn't know what was expected of her and perhaps in truth... neither did Sal?

And that's how they left it.

And so as Sal got ready and laid her new clothes over the back of the armchair Anne hardly moved, she just lay there on the bed Sally's coat pressed against her body, calmer quieter tears now trickling slowly down her cheeks. Sal chatted away to her but Anne never replied. Sally had picked up a pair of red slim high-heeled shoes in a second hand shop in town to complete her outfit and proceeded to twirl this way and that on the balls of her feet observing herself carefully in the long mirror watching the black velvet skirt gather momentum as she moved and admired the way it swirled madly around her legs with every twist. The transformation was truly amazing and when she was finished she didn't look anything like the schoolgirl she'd been only a few months earlier. In fact she didn't look like anyone that Anne had ever seen before and certainly not in Chorley apart from the classy models she'd seen pictures of in some of the high-end fashion magazines that somehow eventually had found their way into the local hairdressers usually six months out of date. Sal appeared at least ten years older than she actually was, a sophisticated beautiful young woman who would not look out of place on the Paris catwalk. A complex and beguiling creature that very soon would arrive at Tom Smith's impressive country house and literally knock him off his feet.

Despite the fact she was loath to see Sally go inevitably it was Anne who slipped downstairs to use her dad's telephone to phone for a taxi, and though it broke her heart to do so, she obeyed Sal's wishes right up until the end. What else could she do? Sally would not be dictated to by anyone. If Bob Fraser a guy who even his daughter considered a psychopath was unable to restrain his willful offspring then poor little Anne Turner was on a hiding to nothing. No... she would have to let her go and then one day when she was ready... her friend would return... she was sure.

And then predictably as the cab pulled up outside Anne grabbed hold of Sal's bag without even thinking about it, faithful as ever, but noticing immediately how heavy it was for just an overnight stay. She didn't dare to say anything, why would she? The two friends hugged for a brief moment... perhaps slightly longer than usual but then finally as Sal climbed in to the car and she turned back to face Anne for the very last time a huge smile radiated across her face.

"Don't worry." Sally whispered. "I'll be fine!"

Chapter 12

It was dusk as the cab headed east out of town and up Stump Lane. Sal was too preoccupied fumbling around inside her overnight bag to notice several other vehicles close behind, one of them a familiar powder blue color not dissimilar to Jerry Thompson's motor or come to that Bob Fraser's family saloon. But as soon as the taxi driver put his foot on the pedal and headed off into the hills towards Rivington it appeared finally that they were on their own. Fifteen minutes later they pulled off the road completely and took a sharp left into Fred Smith's driveway and as the cab came to a halt outside the property Tom came out to meet her. He was dressed in cream flannel trousers and a pale green short-sleeved shirt. His thick black hair combed right back from a high forehead noticeably long at the back and hanging down onto his shoulders… needless to say he looked very cool and very, very handsome.

"Wow… Sal!" Tom gasped as she stepped away from the car. "You look fabulous."

She smiled nervously taken aback somewhat by this sudden attention and there was a flicker of concern in her face that did not go unnoticed until once again she managed to compose herself and Sal's normal detachment resumed.

"Thanks." She whispered. "And you Tom… you don't look too bad either… you've scrubbed up well." And then she noticed what looked like a number of bright red scratches on both of his arms. "Although it looks like you might have scrubbed a bit too hard." She added.

Tom glanced down and reexamined his recent cuts. "Oh yeah." He smiled. "That… that's nothing… I've been cutting all the hedges for the old fella and maybe I should have worn something with a bit more protection."

And then without ado… he grabbed her bag.

"Please." He said reassuringly. "Do… come in and welcome to my home."

Sally walked slowly inside the house acutely aware of Tom's every move as he was of hers.

"Right then…first of all Sal…" He asked very politely. "… Would you like a tour?"

"Well… I guess that all depends…?" She smiled.

"On what?"

"On whom else you've invited over?" She asked. "Perhaps we should wait for them and you can show us all round together."

"What…?" He sounded genuinely surprised that she'd even think that anyone else might be joining them. "There is no one else."

"Oh… okay then." Sal grinned. "Then I can only imagine how lonely you'd have been up here all by yourself… if I hadn't of turned up."

"But you were always going to come… weren't you… anyway I never doubted it?" Tom insisted. Not even for a minute… but listen… I need to ask you Sally… do you swim?"

"Yeah… I can swim." Said Sal convincingly. "But why do you ask…?"

"I only wondered." He sighed. "…Because you see… the thing is we've got a great pool here… and it hardly ever gets used."

"So…" Sneered Sally. "…You invited me all the way up here just for a swim?"

"If you like." He said encouragingly.

"No I don't think so." She snapped. "That's not really what I had in mind."

"Well not to worry." He said immediately. "There are loads of other things we can do. But please… let me show you round."

"Okay…" Sally agreed despite her growing unease. "You go ahead Tom and lead the way… I'll follow."

And so he showed Sally the whole of the ground floor including predictably the twenty-meter pool and Fred's garage where his dad housed his collection of old vehicles one of which Tom declared was a 1936 Bugatti road car. It had a 3.3-liter engine with a top speed of 95 miles per hour. A motorcar with a huge history and a thing of beauty, it had dazzling coachwork in green and black and despite being only forty years old Tom insisted. "Was worth an absolute fortune."

The garage was one area where Mavis Smith never ventured but her special touch was evident everywhere else in the house. Beautiful country furniture and endless accessories were abundant in every room. She had a huge kitchen with oak beams and Italian tiles and every appliance that could possibly be purchased in 1976.

They wandered upstairs to view the bedrooms and countless bathrooms before finally retiring back to the ground floor and into the very same room where Susie had spent her last night on the moors all those weeks ago. Surrounded by all the same wonderful furnishings and vibrant colors of red, orange and gold that Sal's sister had seen and loved and thought at first that maybe one day she could own. They sat down on the couch across from the French doors, spectacular views ahead of them observing the clouds as they raced by in an easterly direction across the moors. Their ever changing shapes seemingly ominous and threatening but at the same time magnificent to watch.

"So…" Tom whispered. "What do you think… do you like it?"

"Oh … yeah I like it." Sally grinned. "I'd be crazy if I didn't. But you must understand Tom… this is so far removed from the place that I was reared its hard to believe that some people live like this."

"Well… tell me if I'm mistaken Sal." Tom insisted. "But your big sister now lives in a fine house in the country… does she not?"

Sally glared at the guy. Any mention of Susie was always certain to get a reaction but when someone praised her big sister for anything she'd done or achieved it goaded Sal… it always had!

"I agree… Susie's house is lovely." She conceded. "But its nothing on the scale of this place. This is something else."

"Exactly!" Said Tom emphatically. "So there you go then. This could all be yours and you could go one better… a lot better. Think about it."

Sally's stare got even more intense. She was up on the Pennine moors and miles from anywhere alone with a guy she hardly knew. A man who appeared very normal but in truth was unreal, unhinged maybe and who whether he realized it or not had a huge obsession with one or perhaps both of the Fraser girls.

"Why Tom?' Sally asked suddenly. "Why…?"

"Why what?" He looked upset.

"Why me?" She answered. "Its Susie you really wanted isn't it… why don't you admit it?"

"No its not." He insisted. "Its you Sal… I don't care about Susie… honest!"

"I don't believe you Tom." Sally shouted. "And if there's one thing I won't do is to play second fiddle to anyone... especially Susie."

"You don't have to Sal..." He begged her. "It was you I always wanted. I only used her to get to you... I swear. You've got to believe me. My old fella won't be around forever and when he moves on, this place will be ours... yours and mine. Think about it!"

Sally didn't answer. She didn't need to. She knew what she had to do.

I'll tell you what I would like Tom." Sally said eventually.

"What?" He replied.

"A drink maybe?" She suggested.

"Of course." He said. "Yeah... I'm sorry... I got carried away. I should have offered you one when you first arrived. What can I get you?"

"Brandy and coke." Sally grinned mischievously. "That's what you normally have... isn't it?"

"Yeah you're right." He said. "...You've a good memory lass."

Tom disappeared immediately into the kitchen. He was desperate to impress her and the harder Sal made it for him and the more his influence waivered the more he wanted her. By the time he returned Sal had opened her overnight bag and was reapplying her lippy, a deliberate sensuous and provocative act that she performed with the utmost dexterity. When Tom noticed what she was doing he froze on the spot appearing very much like a rabbit caught in the headlights.

"Thanks Tom." She said sweetly as he passed her the glass. "But could I possibly have some more ice in there please?"

"Yeah... no problem." Tom smiled.

He placed his own glass on the coffee table and went back into the kitchen with Sally's. It didn't take him long but it was all she needed... by the time he'd returned... the deed was done.

For a moment or two she appeared quite nervous but as Tom took a huge gulp of his drink and slumped back in his seat Sally began very gradually to breath a lot easier and as the conversation continued she relaxed completely for the first time that day.

"I didn't thank you did I Tom?" Sally announced. "For the gifts."

There was no doubt Tom could definitely hear what she'd said but all of a sudden he'd acquired a strange vacant expression on his face and he looked quite weary.

"The jewelry!" Sally pushed him for an answer. "It was very kind of you?"

"Yeah... of course Sal." He replied trying his best to keep in touch. "No problem."

"It must have cost you a fortune?"

"What's that then?"

"The things you bought for me?" Sally insisted. "You spent a lot of money?"

"Did I?"

"Yes you did Tom." Sally leaned in towards him. "…And I'm very grateful."

"That's good… that's really good." He slurred.

"Now listen to me… I need to ask you something." Sal snapped. "Are you listening Tom?"

"Yeah… I'm listening." Tom barked as he gulped down the remainder of his brandy and sat back even further until he was almost horizontal.

"When Susie came here." Sally goaded him. "Do you remember that?"

"Of course." Tom seemed to rally somewhat. "… Of course I do."

"Well the thing is… Susie thinks you drugged her and took advantage of her … did you?"

Tom looked horrified.

"Did you?" Sally screamed at him only inches from his face. "Did you Tom?"

"No!" He cried. "No, No, No… I didn't do that… I wouldn't would I?"

"Why Tom…?" Sal shouted. Why should I believe you… why?"

"Because…" He cried. "…Because I love her!"

From that moment on any sympathy that Sal might have had for the pretty rich boy that lived up on the hill disappeared completely. Tom Smith and every other bloke that had used her and abused her would pay the price. He'd lied to her just like all the others and Sal had an answer for that.

"No… don't worry Tom." Sally whispered in his ear as she began to stroke his hair very, very gently. "…I know you didn't do that."

"No… no I didn't." He muttered still struggling with his speech, his words now almost unintelligible.

"I know." She said. "Because I know what happened."

Tom looked like he'd given up altogether he was dazed and confused and almost flat on his back. In a few minutes he'd be unconscious and so she grabbed him by his shoulders and shook him forcefully in order to make him listen.

"I did it…" She screamed loudly. "Yes… me! I've been here before Tom in this very same room. On the last night when Susie stayed here, you poured her a nightcap… remember?"

"… Remember!" Was all Tom could mutter and even though she knew what he was trying to say that one single word was almost unrecognizable.

"There's a drug." Sal announced suddenly. "You've probably never heard of it…its called flunitrazepam… its a strange name isn't it Tom?"

Tom was almost comatose and so she slapped him really hard across the face numerous times in order to get his attention and for a moment at least it did appear to work as it shocked him into action and hauled him out of his stupor.

"Yeah…" She bawled at him as loudly as she possibly could. "And that's what I put in Susie's drink… and surprise, surprise Tom that's what you've just had. Exactly the same substance, but don't worry… you won't remember any of this in the morning… I promise!"

And that was the very last word that she intended to say to him.

She allowed him to collapse completely onto the couch and went about her business in and around the house. It took her a while to get organized and to do all the things she needed to do but then finally as she prepared to leave she popped her head back around the huge doorframe one last time… just to check that he was still fast asleep.

But when she looked… he was gone!

Chapter 13

When Harry Sutcliffe turned up at Chorley Police Station on Sunday night he seemed unmoved by anxiety and talked quite cheerfully about his missing daughter. He was a bald man with a deep voice and a roll of fat around his neck that all but obscured his stiff white collar.

"The thing is." He said numerous times. "She's gone AWOL before, but not for this long."

"So tell me Mister Sutcliffe exactly when did you last see Maggie?" The young constable on the desk smiled reassuringly, he was pretty chilled having only just started his shift ten minutes earlier. He'd had plenty of experience already helping to track people down in the past, in particular teenagers after their parents or friends had reported them missing. And usually, in fact almost always, the kid turned up a few days later no worse for wear having used up lots of police time and resources after a completely pointless exercise.

"Last Tuesday... I reckon." Harry answered eventually.

PC John Fairclough placed his pen down on the counter and looked at the man with a fair degree of cynicism. "Last Tuesday?" He said. "... Five days ago... is that correct?"

"Yeah... I suppose so?" Harry agreed.

"It is important Sir... we need to know." Said the young copper.

"I don't know for sure." Harry insisted. "It was either Monday or Tuesday... something like that."

"And you didn't think to let us know before now... eh?"

"I'm not that worried." Harry stressed. "Like I say... she's done this before."

"Right." Said the PC as he got reacquainted with his biro. "I'll need some details... yours and Maggie's!"

And then in the early hours of Monday morning it was Pat Fraser's turn to put in an appearance at the very same Police Station. The young bobby had only just completed all the paper work regarding the missing young woman... "Maggie Sutcliffe." When all of a sudden he was faced with yet another disappearance, that of "Sally Fraser."

When Sal hadn't returned home from her friend's house on Sunday evening her mum had walked across town to Anne Turner's house to see where she was. Pat hadn't seen Sally or Bob come to that for almost thirty-six hours. Shortly after his big row with Sally he'd taken a phone call jumped in the car and drove off immediately, but he was the last of Pat's worries. At first ever loyal Anne wouldn't say anything but then eventually under pressure from both Sal's mum and her own parents she'd given in and told them what she knew. Anne's dad had offered to drive up on to the moors and consequently both he and Pat Fraser had travelled directly to Tom's place in order to try and find her. But despite being able to pull into the driveway of Fred Smith's property and walk around the gardens, any access to the house itself had been impossible. There was no answer at any of the doors and no sign of life. All the downstairs drapes had been closed so apart from breaking in and forcing entry it left them few options. It was something that Jimmy Turner had considered very seriously but quickly changed his mind when he remembered how influential Fred Smith could be and there was always the small matter of Fred's account at the builders merchants that Jim worked for over in Leyland. One rash silly initiative on his part could jeopardize everything and the more he thought about it the more he decided against it.

They drove back into town and immediately began to telephone anyone that Pat could possibly think of, anyone who might throw some light on Sally's sudden disappearance. Almost everyone she phoned was sympathetic but every call drew a blank. There was one recipient however who listened intently to what was being said but didn't offer any words of reassurance and that was Susie. Pats eldest daughter now at least half way through her pregnancy was ready for bed when the phone rang and as Pat had already correctly assumed, Susie had no idea where Sally might be. The two sisters barely spoke to each other these days and in fact by the time she'd made this particular call, Pat was clutching at straws. Although what Pat didn't know was that

Sally's disappearance posed even more of a problem for her eldest daughter than what she could ever imagine. Pat was totally unaware of what had gone on at the cottage with Sal and Jerry a few days earlier, unlike Susie of course. But given the news about Sally, it begged the question where the hell was Jerry Thompson, because Susie hadn't heard from him since late on Saturday afternoon when Jerry called her from the office, he'd been invited away at short notice by a guy in the Lakes who wanted him to market a number of apartments for him in Bowness on Windermere? At the time Susie did wonder if he was telling the truth but didn't really care, after what had happened in recent days the least she saw of Jerry's ugly mug the better and it had given her more time to consider her options.

"If I hear anything mum." Said Susie calmly. "I will let you know… okay?" And then she put the phone down immediately and went to bed.

And so… three hours later with no other leads to work on, at the end of her tether and with no husband there to support her, Pat decided that she had little or no alternative but to get the police involved.

PC John Fairclough was a lot busier than he would have normally expected for a Sunday night but two young women reported missing within such a short period of time was needless to say an unusual event and it was therefore a night he would never forget.

Harry Sutcliffe and Pat Fraser were shown to two separate rooms at the station and had no interaction. They were however interviewed by the same officers whose first thoughts were that the two missing girls might be friends and that their disappearances were in some way connected. The two parents had never met nor had they any knowledge of each other but when informed that there were in fact two girls that had disappeared, both were asked the same question.

"Do you know the other missing girl?"

In both cases the answer was surprisingly… exactly the same. "No!"

Sally's disappearance was a little more concerning but only because she was under eighteen and at twenty-four years of age Maggie Sutcliffe's case was certainly not considered too worrying. That however was due to in part to Harry's very languid and relaxed way in which he'd reported his daughter missing when he'd first entered the station. If he wasn't taking the matter seriously then it was pretty obvious that the coppers wouldn't be too alarmed either. After all the statistics spoke for themselves. Most missing persons turned up within twenty-four hours and when the police decided that these two new cases were to be considered "low risk" it was only a matter of time before they expected that both of these parents would be reunited with their kids. There was one other factor that had helped to convince the cops that in the case of the missing teenager Sally Fraser there could be a very good reason why she hadn't returned home and that was due to comments made by one of the old bobbies on duty that night namely sergeant Sam Bradshaw who knew the Fraser's. Or to be more precise he known all about the girls father twenty odd years ago when Bob came back from Korea. Sam didn't like Bob Fraser and he was well aware of what the ex-serviceman and so called war hero had done to his family, how he'd abused them and how he'd subjected Pat to all kinds of physical and mental torture. The sergeant had suggested to the other boys in blue that they should consider Sally's disappearance as an indication of a problem in her life rather than an event in itself.

"If Bob Fraser was my old fella." He growled. "I'd have left home a long time ago."

And therefore in the absence of any other contributory factors such as problems with sexuality, religious issues or ethnicity the police's first response was mediocre to say the least. Pat was asked to give the police a full description of how Sal was dressed when she'd last seen her, a list of all her usual haunts and another list of all her daughters friends with as many contact details as she could remember. Harry Sutcliffe was also asked for the same information about Maggie's friends and where she could normally be found but needless to say his response was not as promising. Eventually it was suggested to both Pat Fraser and Harry Sutcliffe that they should return home and wait there for further news, which was what Harry did straight away. For Pat Fraser however the obvious lack of progress was hard to accept and so before she left the station she insisted on speaking to the sergeant one last time to put her mind at rest that everything that could be done, would be done.

Sam Bradshaw was old school. Unusually small for a policeman, a grey-haired man in a neat uniform who despite his size could appear quite irascible and often heard shouting and giving orders to the younger bobbies. But when he needed it, he had the policeman's perfect equivalent to the doctor's bedside manner, what the traffic cops would refer to when they pulled up a seventy-year old great grandmother for speeding as their roadside manner.

He smiled at Pat and laid a hand reassuringly on her shoulder.

"She'll be fine." He nodded. "I promise… she'll be back before you know it."

"I hope so." Said Pat gratefully. "God… I do hope so."

"Where's Bob by the way?" The policeman asked suddenly. "Is he not worried?"

"You know him Sam." Pat grimaced. "Only cares about himself."

"He's got nothing to do with Sal's disappearance?" Whispered the copper. "… Has he Pat?"

"No sergeant." Pat was adamant. "If he had… I'd be the first to tell you… have no fear about that."

"I know love." He assured her. "I had to ask… you understand?'

"Yeah…" Pat nodded a little and smiled. "I understand."

"Anyway lets get you home." He added. "And I know it's difficult… but when you get back… try and sleep. Come on I'll grab a patrol car and take you myself."

"Thank you Sam." Pat sighed. "But I can't sleep…not until she's back. And please whatever you do, go back to Tom Smiths place will you and see what he has to say for himself… he must know something?"

"We will Pat." The sergeant smiled. "I promise… at first light… we'll send a car."

Chapter 14

When Jerry arrived back at the cottage around five in the morning it was still dark. Susie listened intently whilst he showered and got changed but it was only when she heard him go back downstairs and put the kettle on that she came down herself in order to speak with him.

"So…" Said Susie curiously. "How was your trip?"

Jerry moved forward to try and kiss her on the cheek but Susie slipped away to one side very conveniently and avoided his touch.

"Okay… I guess." He answered rather hesitantly feeling more than a little dejected by Susie's body language and her unwillingness to make contact. "It was definitely worth the effort… but I'll need to cut our margins if we want the business, that's for sure."

"And will you?" Growled Susie.

Jerry was still stinging from his wife's undeniable rejection and because he was tired he couldn't quite grasp Susie's sudden intrusion.

"Will I… Will I what?" He asked as if he'd already forgotten what he was trying to say.

"Will you cut the margins…?" She said brusquely. "You just said you'd have to cut them… to get the business… so will you?"

"Yeah… yeah I guess so. I'll have to work on it." He insisted. "Play around with the figures. You know what I mean?"

"And where did you stay?" Susie snapped.

"At the clients place in Grasmere." Jerry responded quickly. "It was beautiful… you'd have loved it Susan."

And then he continued with even more details about the location of where he'd stayed and what he'd seen. It was either all completely true or a clever fabrication that Jerry had orchestrated and then practiced on his journey home. She realised from the far-away look on his face that his mind was elsewhere and that all he was trying to do was keep her distracted and she wondered how he would react to the news of Sally's disappearance. And then it occurred to her that quite possibly, he might already know. Why she should think that she wasn't quite sure but Susie knew all too well that there'd be more to Jerry's weekend away than what he would pretend. He couldn't be trusted, she knew that now and despite her relief and satisfaction a few months earlier when she'd got married, moved away to the country and escaped the dangerous clutches of her father. She was now very aware that all she'd really done was to exchange one dominating and scheming alpha male for a slightly younger richer model.

She's Missing

Susie stood rooted to the spot her brain trying hard to make sense of the nonsense her life and increasingly strained relationship with Jerry Thompson had become. She forced her eyes away from his and sat down. Jerry placed his cup on the table and sat down across from her an expectant look etched across his face.

"You want to say something Susan?" He said quite aggressively as if suddenly he was looking for a quarrel.

"She's missing...?" Susie answered him straight away.

"What?" Said Jerry. "What are you talking about?"

"Sally!" Said Susie. "...She's gone missing!"

It wasn't often that Jerry Thompson was caught unawares but it did appear as if Susie's comment had more than ruffled his feathers. His face reddened and suddenly he became quiet agitated, obviously confused by this new turn of events.

"When?" He stuttered. "When was this?"

"On Saturday apparently." Said Susie assertively. "Two days ago... whilst you were away?"

"So...?" Said Jerry trying his best to act normal as if nothing had knocked him off his stride. "Where will she have gone... do you reckon?"

"If they knew that." Said Susie. "They wouldn't be out there looking for her... would they?"

"They…?" Said Jerry pensively. "Who are they?"

"The police I presume." Said Susie. "That's where mum was headed last night when I last spoke to her."

"Sounds a bit drastic?" Said Jerry.

"Really… is that what you think?" Said Susie. "She's only sixteen and she's not been seen for almost two days. If she was your daughter Jerry… what would you do?"

"I don't know." Jerry muttered. "I don't know what I'd do. But lets face it she is a bit wild… unpredictable."

"Yeah maybe." Said Susie very deliberately. "But you can't ignore the fact that no one knows where she is and there are lots of people out there that might take advantage of her. Can't you see that Jerry?"

Jerry didn't know what to say. He'd said too much already and so he got to his feet sidled across to the sink and rinsed his cup under the tap. Then all of a sudden he stepped back towards her, his eyes weirdly fixated and dared to lay a hand possessively on her shoulder as if he'd listened to enough of what she had to say and intended to regain the initiative. But what he hadn't expected was Susie recoiling in horror and then on cue either as a result of Jerry's impromptu intervention or probably more than likely due to Susie's fragile condition, she was physically sick… all over the table.

When the cop car rolled up outside Pat's house Bob Fraser's motor was already there its two nearside wheels parked up on the curb. Within seconds the lounge curtains were tugged unceremoniously to one side and Bob's head poked through the gap in order for him to determine who'd dared to park anywhere near his property.

And as the police vehicle came to a standstill Bob was already in the street eager to know why his wife had been brought home by the local constabulary and find out what the hell was happening.

Sam Bradshaw wound the driver's window down immediately and stopped the engine.

"Evening Bob." Said the sergeant sounding very pragmatic. "So… is she back by any chance?"

"Who?" Bob barked as surly as ever. "Whom are we talking about?"

"Sally… your daughter." Said the copper. "She's missing?"

"Missing?" Bob snarled. "What do you mean… missing?"

"Missing." Said sergeant Bradshaw. "… As in… we don't know where she is. Your good lady here has reported her missing… and now we're looking for her. So if there's anything you can tell us Bob. We'd be very grateful okay?"

Suddenly it dawned on Bob who the officer was. He was the nosy copper who wanted Pat to bring charges against him almost twenty years ago and when she wouldn't, he hassled Bob for months on end and tried to get him locked up for all sorts of other misdemeanors.

As far as Bob Fraser was concerned all the boys in blue were trouble but this particular cop had been a real pain in the ass and Bob knew all too well that if he didn't watch his step sergeant Bradshaw would give him some serious grief.

"No." Said Bob sounding slightly more respectful. "No... she's not here."

Pat clambered out of the vehicle, shut the car door behind her and turned to face the policeman.

"Thank you sergeant." She whispered. "I'll phone you straight away if Sally gets in touch okay?"

"Yes... do that." He smiled. "And... Pat... Listen please if you need us at all... for anything. Just phone us or come back in to the station. We're always there twenty four seven... you know that don't you? We'll be in touch!"

Pat never even looked at Bob as she brushed by him and walked up the path and into the house. Meanwhile the two men just stared at one another, weighing each other up, remembering the past and more importantly considering their next move.

"By the way Bob." Said the sergeant as he turned the ignition key very, very slowly. "If I'm not mistaken... that looks like your motor over there... and as far as I can see it's illegally parked. Now the thing is Bob you're not allowed to park on the curb because it obstructs the pathway and as you can imagine that's a danger to pedestrians. Just think about it... in a few months time when your lovely Susie is pushing your first grandchild up and down the street you wouldn't want her to have to push the child in the road with all that traffic now would you? Have some consideration man... otherwise I'll have to book you... understand?"

"No worries officer... I understand." Bob growled sarcastically "And thank you for the advice... you've obviously kept yourself very well informed."

"Yeah... that's what we do." Said the sergeant. "In case you didn't know...we look out for people and in particular those at risk... so make sure you don't forget that... will you Bob... we'll need to speak with you again a little later?"

And with those final chilling words ringing in his ears Bob Fraser watched intently as the cop car drove away and disappeared into the night.

Chapter 15

At daybreak exactly as sergeant Bradshaw had promised a police patrol car pulled into the driveway that led to Fred Smiths expansive property. PC John Fairclough the young cop who'd been on the desk the previous evening was dog tired and at the end of his shift, he was accompanied by another rookie whose job it was to try and speak to Tom Smith and see what he knew about Sally Fraser's disappearance. They walked around the house several times very much like Pat and Annie's dad had done previously, knocked on all the doors and windows and tried unsuccessfully to peep through the downstairs drapes. But despite their efforts it was a fruitless exercise and after reporting in by radio they were called back to the station to deal with other matters.

And only as they turned the car around and headed off away from the property when Fairclough grabbed a last look towards the house did he suspect that there might just be someone at home after all.

"Stop right there…." He shouted to his driver. "…There's someone upstairs."

His colleague wasn't convinced although he didn't hesitate and once more they parked the patrol car and walked back. They banged ever harder on the windows and doors and even shouted through the letterbox but still there was no answer.

"I'd swear I saw somebody." Insisted the young cop. "By the window… I saw the curtains move… definitely."

"I don't think so John." Sighed his partner. "You're tired mate that's all… come on lets get back to the station… you need to clock off. The other lads will chase the guy down sooner or later you can be sure of that."

So once again assuming that Tom Smith was still at home the good looking rich kid had remained ever elusive and almost two days since Sally's visit he'd avoided being seen.

By lunchtime on Monday and with growing concerns about the girl's safety the police efforts were slowly but surely ratcheted up a notch and Annie Turner was asked if she would attend the police station with at least one of her parents. At sixteen she could not be interviewed without one of them being present and therefore Annie and her mum made their way across town to see if they could help.

The girl took some convincing that she should tell them everything about Sal, someone whose interests she had protected faithfully since childhood. Even discussing her friend with strangers made Anne feel uncomfortable and if there was one thing she knew about Sally it was Sal's obsession with keeping secrets and her uncompromising attitude towards any sort of disloyalty. Persuaded by her mother she eventually gave the police a time line from when Sal arrived at her house on Saturday afternoon until the taxi picked her up and transported her to Tom Smith's house a few hours later. The most interesting thing for the police was this latest description of the missing girl and what she'd apparently been wearing when she left Anne Turners house. It was totally different from the description that Pat had given them the previous evening and by all accounts the clothes that Sal had been asked to wear by Tom Smith would not be hard to recognize nor would there be many like them certainly in a northern working class town like Chorley.

But as resources increased in order to try and resolve the question of where they might be, the mystery deepened and now almost two days on, there was still no sign of either girl.

Once police started their enquiries in the bars and pubs and spoke to other young people in the borough they soon realised that Maggie Sutcliffe was widely known and not always for the right reasons. A number of those they interviewed described her as warm with a lively spirit but someone who could be rather earthy and all too willing to jump into bed with numerous casual acquaintances.

In police opinion a recipe for disaster.

On the one hand she appeared quite shameless but at the same time very vulnerable and a young woman in desperate need of a proper friend and loyal companion. One landlord was scathing when the bobby's questioned him about Maggie but most of the criticism was directed at her father as opposed to the girl herself. Harry Sutcliffe had apparently neglected the girl for the last twenty years. When his wife died in nineteen fifty-six he'd gone completely off the rails and didn't have a clue how to raise the young lass. Social Services had considered taking her into care but every time they voiced their concerns Harry would obstruct them at every opportunity and even introduced a number of what turned out to be very questionable women who he claimed would help him look after the child. Things would usually improve for a short while at least and Maggie would turn up at school a bit smarter and thankfully not as smelly. But then eventually her appearance would deteriorate and once again she'd be the kid that no one wanted to sit next to.

By the time she'd got into her teens it was too late for anyone to do anything to really help her. The girl was streetwise and yes she'd learned to survive but some of things she'd had to do were undoubtedly perverse and inappropriate.

In other words exactly like Sally Fraser who could be excused for not wanting to go home to an abusive parent, Maggie Sutcliffe also had good reason for never wanting to set foot in her dad's house ever again. Were the two disappearances connected in some way? At this stage in the investigation, the police had no way of knowing.

At three o'clock on Monday afternoon yet another much larger more substantial police car drove out of Chorley town center and made its way up onto the West Pennine Moors. Detective Inspector Peter Franks had travelled over from Manchester in his Rover 3500 with its powerful V8 engine and top speed of one hundred and twenty five miles an hour. The sudden disappearance of two young girls was now considered a serious matter with the risk factor now increased to a status of "medium" and Franks or "Franco" as he was affectionately known by his men was now in charge of the search for both girls. He was forty years of age and of ample proportions, his loose brown linen suit accentuating his bulk. His hair was so black he appeared at least ten years younger but noticeably for a copper it was quite long and so he swept it back away from his fleshy almost arrogant face. With his tiny moustache he looked very much like a larger version of "El Caudillo" namely Franco, the repressive dictator of Spain who'd only just died the previous year.

Immediately they pulled up outside Fred Smith's house he climbed out of the car and walked across the grass with detective sergeant Sumner. The two police officers approached the house like men on a mission fiercely determined to get results and if there was one thing that D. I. Franks was used to, it was getting his own way. The young detective sergeant hammered on the door in earnest until it was obvious that he needed to try another approach. He walked back to the motor rather briskly and switched on the police siren. The noise was ear shattering and if anyone was at home, unless of course they happened to be completely deaf, they couldn't fail to hear the unwanted commotion outside. The alarm echoed all around the property and across the open moorland, a seriously unpleasant sound reverberating along the hillside. And if there was one particular thing the experts had proven could raise the blood pressure or raise the dead even, it had to be this.

And amazingly as if by magic the door to the main house opened wide and Tom Smith staggered out looking completely and utterly knackered. The guy was still dressed in the same cream flannel trousers and pale green shirt that he'd worn on Saturday evening but now they looked more like rags as if he'd slept in them for the past two days and nights and if the D.I. wasn't mistaken a lot more beside.

When he spoke to the kid it was straight to the point. "Are you Tom Smith?" He growled. "…Yes or no?"

Tom just stared straight ahead a pathetic vacant expression on his face and even though he tried, he looked completely incapable of answering the Inspector's question in any sort of meaningful way. Tears began trickling uncontrollably down Tom Smith's cheeks until eventually he collapsed on the floor in a heap and blubbered like a baby.

"I'll take that as a yes." Insisted the D.I. as he brushed him by and stepped inside the house. "Okay Tom…you can follow me." He added. "And if you've got any sense lad… you better start talking!"

Tom glared at him in silence but did what he was told.

As the two policemen soon observed, the house although extremely palatial was an awful mess. There were several items of furniture either on their side or evidently out of place and a number of Mavis's beautiful vases had crashed to the ground their remains and contents strewn across the floor. It was dark and gloomy and the whole place smelled like what you might expect in a city center public toilet.

"Lets get those drapes open shall we sergeant." The D.I. insisted. "And for god's sake man open some windows as well…it reeks in here."

"Yes boss." Said sergeant Sumner. "I'm on it right away."

"What do you want?" Tom suddenly demanded. "Why are you people even here?"

"That's a good question Tom." Said the D.I. "Cause I can think of lots of other places I'd rather be right now and this house really stinks… do you know that?"

Tom hesitated then nodded.

"This is your Dad's place isn't it?" Asked the Inspector calmly.

Tom nodded yet again.

"So… when is he back?"

"Tomorrow!" Said Tom hoarsely.

"Tomorrow…?" Said the D.I. sounding mildly sympathetic. "You'll have to get your skates on Tom if you're going to clean this place up in time?"

Tom Smith still looked dazed… bewildered almost. He was gradually regaining his senses but not fast enough for D.I. Franks. The Inspector had a job to do and he intended to get it done one way or another. He waved the sergeant over and whispered in his ear, there was a sense of urgency in his voice that his colleague recognized straight away but despite this Tom had no idea what the D.I. intended. And as Franks began to speak once more the young sergeant slipped away to see what he could find?

"You have a lot of scratches on your arms Tom?" Said the policeman. "… What happened?"

"I don't know?' Tom mumbled. "I've no idea… shit happens doesn't it?"

"Well it does to some people." The D.I. sneered. "… Evidently!"

"I can't remember." Tom insisted.

"And I'd be almost certain that you don't know what day it is…do you lad?" The Inspector snapped.

Tom appeared flummoxed and by the look on his face the cop had him over a barrel. The truth was, Tom wasn't even sure what planet he was on.

"Sunday…!" Tom insisted suddenly. "It's Sunday!"

"Okay…." The D.I. humored him. "So…if that's what you reckon. What about yesterday?"

"Yesterday?" Asked Tom desperately.

"Yeah." The D.I. challenged him. "If today's Sunday… then what the hell happened to you on

Saturday... to leave you in such a mess. Who did you see Tom... anyone?"

Tom Smith's head was spinning. The guy was in turmoil. He wasn't trying to be obstructive he really genuinely could not remember a thing.

"Did somebody come here Tom?" The Inspector growled. "...Is that what happened?"

Tom gazed straight ahead his eyes had glassed over.

"Who was it Tom?" Said the D.I. angrily. "... A girl?"

Tom started crying yet again he wanted to remember and then shout back at the smug copper who was giving him so much grief but no matter how hard he tried he was lost.

"It was a girl wasn't it?" Insisted Franks. "...Just say it. We both know it don't we Tom. Come on... out with it?"

"Okay!" Said Tom suddenly. "...It was Sal!"

"Sally Fraser...?" The D.I. smiled.

"Yeah... Sally Fraser!" Tom repeated the name.

There was a long arduous pause that gave the Inspector just a little extra time to consider his next few words very carefully.

"...And where is she now?" The D.I. asked eventually. "...Where is Sally?"

"I don't know." Said Tom painfully. "I don't know… I can't remember!"

Chapter 16

It was late Monday afternoon and still with no word about Sally, Pat was almost at her wits end. Despair flooded over her and so she sat down in Sal's bedroom and opened the bottom drawer in her daughter's wardrobe. She rummaged through all sorts of stuff that Sally had saved, a lot of which meant very little to Pat but needless to say these were items that could have important significance in finding the girl. There were lots of notes and letters, some of them just a jot on the back of a schoolbook and even a beer mat, but a number that had been addressed to Susie as well. Why Sal should have these tucked away with her own correspondence was anyone's guess but as Pat had always been aware, nothing about Sally Fraser was ever straightforward or simple?

Then suddenly among all the letters Pat found probably the most contentious scribble of them all, the note that Tom Smith had sent to Susie on her return from the moors. She read it eagerly with no thoughts whatsoever for Sally's privacy or come to that Susie's either. And as she looked further Pat discovered even more evidence of Tom's strange behavior and subsequently the most damning article of all, namely his second most recent letter... the one addressed to Sally inviting her away for the weekend and his plans for the future.

Pat stuffed the documents into her handbag immediately, grabbed her hat and coat and set off once more for the police station.

And if there was one thing that never changed at the Lancashire constabulary it was the endless amount of paperwork and procedure and based on the previous nights experience Pat was well aware that this next visit could take a while. What she wasn't expecting to see however was Susie's little mini parked up outside the station.

Pat hesitated for a moment wondering if she might be imagining it, but no, it was definitely Susie's car. Two fluffy black and white dice hanging down from the interior mirror and the unmistakable private number plate that Jerry had purchased for her at god knows what sort of exorbitant price on the day they'd been married.

S U S 1 E It couldn't possibly be anyone else.

When Pat first stepped inside and approached the desk nobody recognized her. In fact the young bobby on duty was somewhat slow in responding at all although he did eventually catch her eye and wandered over as if he had all the time in the world.

"Can I help you ma'am?" He asked politely but lazily.

"Is it possible for me to speak with sergeant Bradshaw please?" Pat sounded weary.

"I'm not even sure he's in madam." The young officer answered. "But if you hang on a minute... I'll see if I can find him."

The cop disappeared into the back office behind the main desk and didn't show his sweet little face again for at least five minutes and when he did reappear he was still as lethargic as ever.

"Apparently..." He mumbled frustratingly. "Sergeant Bradshaw is holding an interview and could be a while... can I help?"

"Its Missus Fraser." Pat answered quickly. "I came in last night to report a missing person... my daughter... Sally Fraser!"

Something in Pat's tone alerted him immediately.

"Oh... right." He stuttered. "I'm sorry Missus Fraser." He said apologetically. "I didn't recognize you. Please come this way. I'll find you somewhere to sit until he's free... can I get you a cup of tea?"

"No its fine thank you..." Pat insisted as she pushed herself away from the desk. "I'll just wait for the sergeant if I may... until he's ready."

"Of course... of course." Said the bobby. "Please come this way."

Back on the moors events were moving fast.

D.I. Franks was still trying to make sense of Tom Smith's involvement, if any, in Sally Fraser's disappearance when suddenly detective sergeant

Sumner dashed back into the house following his search of the garage.

"You've got to come and take a look at this boss." He demanded. "…Straight away."

Intuitively Franks turned towards Tom Smith and glared at the guy watching his every move noticing how suddenly his face had flushed with color. He continued to stare at Tom in silence as the sergeant whispered frantically in his ear.

The D.I.'s mouth tightened.

"Now listen lad." He said. "The sergeant here wants me to take a look at something so he's going to keep you company for a while, whilst I'm away. So… just relax for a few minutes and then we can carry on with our conversation a bit later. Okay Tom?"

Tom nodded.

As he stepped inside the huge garage D.I. Franks ran a hand through his huge mop of hair, most importantly he had to observe and make his own assessment of what the sergeant had found but also make sure that he didn't tamper with or contaminate anything that may at some point in the future be used as evidence. The garage itself had a larger square footage available to house Fred's old cars than most people in Chorley had to live in, especially residents of the back to back terraced properties that skirted the old town. A constant reminder of Chorley's recent industrial past and its need for a large workforce to be close at hand to help spin the cotton in what some would describe as the dark satanic mills.

Franks sidled over towards the shiny vehicle that the sergeant had described. A dazzling green and black Bugatti road car with its 3.3 Liter engine and top speed of ninety five miles an hour, it was a beast of a car. The vehicle was unlocked and so as sergeant Sumner had done only a few minutes earlier the D.I. opened the boot and looked inside.

There was a large green fleece tartan blanket that covered the whole of the trunk, its corner still turned back at an angle exactly as the sergeant had left it and underneath a number of ladies garments that he knew his boss would definitely wish to see.

There was a black cotton skirt simply cut at the hips that released into a full circle at about knee height with a flared hem and most recognizable of all, a sheer black silk chiffon top with red polka dots, ruffled sleeves and a long black satin tie. At first glance the clothing matched the description that Annie Turner had given to the police that same day. She'd described to the police exactly what Sally was wearing when she'd jumped in the taxi on Saturday evening and these items had a remarkable resemblance to the outfit that her friend had been wearing.

Franks pulled a pen from his pocket and used it to flick the chiffon top over to try and read the label inside. He didn't want to mess or touch it with his fingers but he wanted to make absolutely sure that what he was looking at was what had been described. His persistence as usual paid off and he could now see without a shadow of a doubt that these were the articles in question. One label read very clearly "Yves Saint Laurent" the other "Made in France."

These were not as D.I. Franks knew all too well a couple of "off the peg" items from the local rag trade and if he had to, he was prepared to bet everything he owned that these could not be found elsewhere in the North West of England and especially in a little market town such as Chorley.

Tom Smith he decided would have to find some answers… and quick!

Franks closed the boot of the car leaving the clothes in situ, had a good nosy around the rest of the garage before eventually wandering back into the main house to continue with his questions. He was certain at this stage in the investigation that Tom Smith was the last person to have spoken with Sally Fraser prior to the girl's disappearance but whether Smith had harmed her in some way Franks couldn't decide. The D.I. had a lot of experience in dealing with all sorts of criminals and deviants and usually he had suspicions about someone even in the early stages of an enquiry, but this guy Tom Smith, he just couldn't weigh him up at all.

Franks sat down across from Tom and smiled.

"Right then…" He snapped. "I'm going to ask you the same question I asked you before. You need to think about it very, very carefully before you answer me… do you understand?"

"Yeah… I understand." Said Tom resignedly.

"Where is Sally?" Franks growled. "Where is she lad…I need to know?"

"I don't know!" Tom shouted immediately. "If I knew I'd tell you wouldn't I… I just don't know… okay?"

The D.I. sighed predictably as if he didn't expect anything else. Tom Smith was either a really good liar who knew the girl's whereabouts all along, an innocent witness caught up in something in which he'd had no control or alternatively the guy was a fruitcake. It was of course quite possible that Smith might be none of the these, although from what Franks had observed so far in the investigations, it did appear to the D.I. that Tom Smith might possibly be under the influence of something or alternatively he might not be what folks in the area would call "A full shilling."

"Well Tom." Said the Inspector. "That leaves me with only one option."

Tom didn't answer.

"I suggest that we go back into Chorley… you and me." Franks insisted. "And we can have another chat down at the station… what do you think?"

"Does that mean I'm under arrest?" Tom said alarmingly.

"No… I don't think so." Said the D.I. "I don't see any need for that… do you… unless of course you want me to arrest you?"

"No… no I don't want that." Said Tom eagerly.

"Well then… let's just take a ride down town… shall we?" Franks smiled. "If anyone asks…we'll just say that you're helping police with their enquiries… okay?"

"Yeah… okay." Tom agreed.

And so as far as police records would state in regard to the sudden disappearance of Sally Fraser, when Tom Smith was invited back to Chorley police station by Detective Inspector Peter Franks he was listed as a witness… unofficially of course he was the prime suspect.

Chapter 17

Pat Fraser looked uncomfortable. She was worrying herself sick about Sally but having just seen Susie's car outside the station she was concerned for her as well. Pat suspected that Susie's visit to Chorley police station might not be related to Sally's disappearance and she hoped that was the case but the longer she waited to see sergeant Bradshaw the more she realized that was just wishful thinking. And as the minutes ticked away ever so slowly she convinced herself that Susie might somehow be involved, who knows she thought, the two girls hated each other, everyone knew that.

The answer came soon enough when Sam Bradshaw walked in the room. He'd concluded his earlier interview and apologized to Pat profusely for keeping her waiting.

"Hello Pat." He said richly. "I'm so sorry. We've been inundated with customers... word travels fast."

"About Sally?" Pat mumbled.

"Yeah about Sally." He agreed. "And the other young woman as well of course. We've never been as busy."

"And have you found her?" Pat asked desperately.

"No… I'm afraid not love." The sergeant answered. "Not yet anyway."

Pat burst into tears. "I've discovered some letters Sam." She cried. "In Sally's bedroom…I think you need to take a look."

Sergeant Bradshaw unfolded the notes very carefully and read each one in turn. He was an old hand at keeping his thoughts to himself his face showed no emotion and when he'd done, you would never have guessed what he was thinking.

He held up one of the pieces of paper and waved it casually in the air.

"This letter Pat…" He asked curiously. "The one addressed to Susie… has Susie ever seen it?"

"I wouldn't know Sam?" Pat answered. "Maybe… I'm not sure… why?"

The sergeant frowned. "Your two lasses Pat." He insisted. "They don't get on very well… do they?"

"Why…who told you that sergeant?" Pat complained. "…Was it Susie?"

The officer reached across the table and grasped Pat's hand reassuringly. "Its no big deal." He said. "A lot of siblings don't see eye to eye. It's nothing new. I see it all the time."

"Well… why don't we ask her?" Said Pat awkwardly. "About the letter…?"

"What's that…?" Said the sergeant.

"I said… why don't we ask her…?" Pat demanded. "Susie's already here isn't she? I've seen her mini parked up outside so can only assume that she's in here somewhere… where is she Sam?"

"Okay… she's here." Said the sergeant. "I won't deny it."

"So… why is she here?" Said Pat. "Is she in trouble?"

"No… she's not in trouble." Sam Bradshaw was adamant. "We just wanted to speak with her that's all. Its just routine… nothing more."

"And the letters?"

"Yeah… the letters." Repeated the sergeant quickly as if he welcomed the opportunity to talk about anything other than Susie's visit. "They might be really useful. I'd like to show them to the man who's now in charge of the investigation… if I may? It's Detective Inspector Franks from Manchester. He's due back at the station very soon… so unless you've any objections… can I hang on to these please?

She nodded. It was too much to take in all at once. Pat was desperate to help the police but wondered now if Susie really was involved with Sally's disappearance and the thought of that awful possibility suddenly consumed her. Losing Sal was traumatic… losing Susie as well would be unbearable.

Pat shrugged her shoulders and sighed loudly. "Can I see her…?"

"Yeah… of course." Said the sergeant as he got to his feet and stepped towards the door. "We're almost done now… just give me a minute Pat… I'll show her in."

It was probably no more than ten minutes at the most but to Pat Fraser it was an eternity and when finally Susie did appear she threw her arms around her eldest daughter as if she hadn't set eyes on the girl for months.

"Are you okay Susie…?" She cried. "…Is everything alright?"

"Everything's fine Mum." Susie insisted. "It's fine…don't worry."

"Are you sure?"

"Yeah… I'm sure." Susie smiled. "Come on… I'll take you home."

Pat stared at the sergeant as if perhaps they needed his permission but it obvious from Sam Bradshaw's manner that wasn't the case. The two women were free to go whenever and wherever they wished but they could see the pitying way in which the old copper looked at them both and that upset Pat terribly. It was as if he wanted to console her in some way but hadn't got a clue what to say or what to do to make things right. And that was the very first time when Pat suddenly realized that actually… she might never see Sally again!

It was hardly worth Pat getting in the car before Susie pulled up outside her house and therefore little opportunity for either of them to say what they wanted. Pat was reluctant to dig too deeply no doubt frightened of what she might discover and Susie seemed disinclined, unwilling almost to share her thoughts. It was strange how both of them had decided not to get into a lengthy discussion and choosing instead to keep a respectful silence with one overriding factor of course and that was Susie's unborn child. In a few short weeks Pat Fraser would be a grandma and neither Susie nor her mum was prepared to risk the baby, it was as simple as that. If things got out of hand who knows what might happen? At some point in the future things could all be sorted out but until the child was safe, it was better to leave things be. What existed was a mutual compassion between mother and daughter developed over many years in the face of adversity and something that only they could possibly understand.

"Mum…?" Susie asked calmly as Pat climbed unceremoniously out of the tiny vehicle. "…If you need anything?"

"I know…" Pat whispered. "I know love… I'll be in touch."

Susie's mini headed off up the street and away from town. She was desperate to get her feet up and the best place to do that was in a lovely cottage up in the hills on the edge of the West Pennine Moors. She'd have the place to herself for the time being at least and by the time she arrived home in the little hamlet of White Coppice, Susie's errant husband Jerry Thompson would no doubt already be in police custody.

She had sergeant Bradshaw's promise on that.

And Sam Bradshaw as Susie already knew was as good as his word. In fact coincidently as the sergeant's patrol car arrived back at the station with Jerry on board, another car arrived at the same time. It was a huge 3.5 Liter Rover with Detective sergeant Sumner at the wheel, Detective Inspector Peter Franks slumped in the rear and his newly acquired witness, one very odd and confused looking young man named Tom Smith sat beside him.

At this stage the two suspects had something very much in common, neither of them was actually under arrest but both individuals had been invited to Chorley police station for a voluntary interview. And it was hard to say really who looked most surprised when they saw each other but before they had chance to communicate, each of them was whisked away to a separate part of the station.

Their demeanor was noticeably different. Jerry Thompson was his usual brash arrogant self apparently unfazed by his trip to the cop shop whereas Tom Smith was just a mere shadow of his former self either gutted by recent events and possibly by what he'd experienced or as D.I. Franks suspected still under the influence, and he looked like shit.

She's Missing

The Inspector decided to let Tom Smith stew for a while under close observation with a view that he might crack completely and then hopefully be prepared to tell them a lot more about Sally's disappearance. Jerry they decided should be interviewed straight away before he kicked off and demanded that they arrest him for something or let him go. And therefore as soon as sergeant Bradshaw had briefed the D.I. on recent developments, Franks introduced himself to Jerry Thompson and began what was in effect an interrogation.

"I take it you've heard the news about your sister in law?" Said the D.I. softly. "…Am I right?"

"Yeah… I've heard." Snapped Jerry harshly.

"So…" Said Franks. "I've got to ask you Jerry… why aren't you out there looking for her like everyone else?"

"I've got a business to run." Growled Jerry. "…People depend on me."

"But she's family?" Insisted the Inspector.

"She's just a stupid kid."

"Yeah you're right…" Said Franks. "A kid… even more reason to be worried about her?"

"She'll be back." Said Jerry confidently. "You'll see…"

"Really." Said Franks. "So how come you're so sure… her mother and sister are worried sick?"

"I doubt it." Jerry smiled. "I reckon secretly… they're probably enjoying the peace and quiet."

"That's a strange thing to say." Insisted the D.I. "The girls sixteen man… for god's sake. Have you no feelings?"

Jerry stared at Franks intently. If he'd wanted to he could have walked there and then. He hadn't been arrested and he hadn't been charged with anything. The boys in blue had asked him to come down to the station and he'd agreed but if this weird looking copper with his funny brown suit and long black hair continued to annoy him any more that's exactly what he would do.

"She's trouble." Jerry sighed loudly. "Sally… she's bad news, trust me."

"Why's that then?" Franks asked.

"She just is…" Said Jerry. "Ask anyone… anyone who knows her… they'll tell you."

"And where were you on Saturday Jerry?" The D.I. said forcefully. "Can you tell me…?"

Jerry delayed proceedings yet again. He didn't appear particularly concerned but he did think long and hard about how he answered.

"Perhaps I need to get myself some representation Inspector?" Jerry asked directly. "What do you think… will that be necessary?"

"If you wish." Franks answered him immediately. "…All we actually wanted was a little chat… but it's entirely up to you."

There was a long silence.

"I was away…" Said Jerry hesitantly. "… On business."

"And where did you get to?" Asked Franks.

"Here and there." Said Jerry. "You know how it is?"

"No… not really." Said the Inspector. "That's why I'm asking."

"New clients." Jerry advised him. "…Up North… wanted me to take a look at some new properties."

"I'll need more than that…" Said Franks.

"Yeah… well… it's not a problem." Insisted Jerry. "I can organize all that for you. Just let me know…?"

"You need an alibi Jerry." Growled the Inspector. "… That's what you need?"

"Why's that then?" Shouted Jerry defiantly. "What am I supposed to have done?"

"I don't know yet?" Snapped Franks. "You tell me."

"I've done nothing." Jerry insisted.

"Okay…" Said the Inspector. "Then I'm sure you won't mind if we take a look in your car?"

"I don't consent to that." Jerry's face reddened.

"Why's that then?" Asked Franks immediately. "What have you got to hide man?"

Jerry got to his feet quickly and almost pushed the table over in the process. He'd heard enough.

"Nothing…" He snarled. "I've got absolutely nothing to hide."

"You're the only person we've interviewed so far?" Franks badgered him. "…Who is being obstructive?"

"Obstructive…?" Yelled Jerry. "What's that supposed to mean?"

The Inspector sighed. "Susie came in to see us a little earlier." He whispered. "She had no problem talking to us!"

"My wife…?" Jerry demanded to know. "You've spoken to my wife?"

"Oh yeah." Said Franks confidently. "We've spoken to her… and lots of other people as well."

"She's almost seven months pregnant!" Jerry shouted.

"I'm well aware of that." Franks agreed. "But still… it didn't stop her talking. In fact she was eager to help us… Sally's her sister you know… have you forgotten that?"

"No...!" Growled Jerry. "I bloody well haven't forgotten... what do you think I am an imbecile?"

"No... you're not an idiot!" Snapped the Inspector. "...But you're acting like one."

Suddenly Jerry slumped back down in the chair and stretched out his legs. He reached down into his trouser pocket and dragged out his car keys, stared at Franks defiantly then threw them carelessly across the table.

"Go ahead..." Said Jerry somewhat despondently. "Do what you wish?"

K. E. Heaton

Chapter 18

Twenty-four hours later both Jerry Thompson and Tom Smith were still helping police with their enquiries… and they weren't alone. In the early hours the cops had picked up Bob Fraser as well and persuaded him to go the station and help in the search for his daughter. He'd gone with them but it was something the ex-soldier appeared very reluctant to do?

D.I. Franks had been keen to speak with Sally's dad anyway but after two of the Fraser's close neighbors had reported the huge argument that had taken place between Sally and her father a few days earlier, it gave the Inspector a legitimate reason to haul the guy in to explain what he'd been up to since his daughters disappearance.

Predictably Bob was his usual truculent self. He was rude, stubborn and uncooperative and the D.I. took an instant dislike to the man.

The interview soon turned sour and before very long the two men were literally at each other's throats.

"Don't you care what's happened to her?" Said the Inspector. "It seems to me like you're glad to see the back of her… is that right?"

"You're talking bollocks man." Said Bob. "So… am I free to go… yes or no?"

"You're not doing yourself any favors… are you?" Franks insisted. "But worse than that you're hindering the investigation."

"I don't see how?" Bob argued.

"Oh yeah definitely." Said the cop. "… You probably haven't thought this through Bob… but I will charge you with a misdemeanor or even felony if you don't change your tune."

Oh yeah…?" Said Bob.

"Yeah!" Insisted Franks. "If I wanted to I could get you banged up for at least two years Bob… we'll throw the book at you. Is that what you want?"

"It's a set up." Bob snarled. "… You can't do that."

"Can't I…?" The D.I. laughed hoarsely. "You better watch me then. You deserve locking up anyway from what I've heard… wife beater!"

Bob appeared dumbstruck. No one outside the family had ever confronted him… not like this. If he'd been in the pub and someone dared to look at him the way the Inspector had, he'd have wasted the guy without even thinking. And Franks was well aware of Bob Fraser's reputation but with two big burly coppers alongside him he'd nothing to fear. He was paid to get results and that's exactly what he intended to do.

"Right then Mister Fraser." Said the D.I. sarcastically. "Now we've got your attention... what about the other girl... how well do you know her?"

"I've not a clue what you're talking about." Insisted Bob.

"Oh... I think you do." Said Franks. "... Maggie Sutcliffe... you know her Bob... Don't kid your self?"

"Are you going to charge me with something Inspector?" Bob snapped. "...Are you?"

"Yeah... definitely." Franks got to his feet and smiled. "You can count on it Bob... but for time being you can sit right there and behave your self. And if you don't... these lads here will give you a lesson in good manners... understand me?"

"Oh yeah..." Bob murmured. "I understand alright... I reckon there's a name for that."

"What's that then...?" Said Franks as he reached the door.

"Police brutality...!" Said Bob. "That's what I would call it."

"No..." Said the Inspector. "Police brutality is when one of our lot doesn't do his job properly and lets a scum bag like you back on the streets to terrorize his wife and kids and all his neighbors. And I won't tolerate that Bob... ever. That's why you're staying here with me... okay?"

The D.I. was briefed once more by others officers before proceeding to the interview room with Jerry Thompson. When he walked in Susie's husband was dozing in the chair or so it appeared and therefore a well-aimed kick against the table leg signaled the Inspector's need to restart the conversation. It wasn't subtle and it wasn't clever but it did have the desired effect and as Jerry rubbed the sleep away from his eyes Franks began again in earnest.

"We've had a look at your car Jerry." Said the Inspector. "It's a nice motor."

"And…?" Jerry mumbled.

"And… it must have cost a fortune." Franks announced. "At least that's what my lads have just suggested."

"I work hard." Said Jerry. "That's all I can say… A man needs a few nice things."

"Then maybe I should think about becoming an estate agent." The D.I. said flippantly. "A coppers pay is obviously piss poor compared to what you guys are earning?"

"I wouldn't know." Said Jerry. "… Can I go yet?"

The Inspector was still browsing through some of the notes that one of the investigation team had handed him before he'd entered the room. He raised his eyebrows slowly and stared at Jerry Thompson with intent. Of the three men currently helping police with their enquiries this guy was the most interesting. He wasn't the best looking geezer that Franks had ever seen but he had managed to pull the most gorgeous girl in town, marry her and then buy the most exquisite picture postcard cottage up in the hills for them to live in. He owned his own successful business in town, employed a handful of local young women to help run the agency and from what the investigation had discovered, didn't owe anyone a penny. It was certainly an achievement for a poor kid from Blackburn but as the D.I. was well aware, what people saw from the outside was often an illusion and somewhere lurking in the shadows was the truth.

And even though Jerry Thompson intrigued him, Franks also found the guy quite irritating. The witness as the D.I. described him still reeked of aftershave even after all those hours in the station and every few minutes would shake his hand routinely from side to side. No doubt reassuring himself of his new found wealth and position as he watched the gold signet bracelet swirl around his wrist in ever increasing circles. Yes the man was confident all right but how would he react when the Inspector told him what they'd found? Franks wondered. He would verbally spar with him until the right moment came along and then when Jerry Thompson least expected it… he'd pounce suddenly… and capture his prey.

"It all depends…" Franks answered eventually.

"On what?" Said Jerry impatiently.

""Well the thing is Jerry…" Said the Inspector. "I would like to release you… but I have a few reservations about what you might do the minute we let you go."

"I'd go straight home for a shower. "Said Jerry. "I stink… you've probably noticed?"

"Yeah I've noticed." Franks smiled. "But you see there you go… already you've presented me with yet another problem."

"How come?" Jerry argued.

"Because Susie doesn't want you back there!" Insisted Franks. "She knows all about you… and what you've been up to."

Jerry hesitated.

"And what's that then?" He said eventually.

"You and Sally." Franks spat the words out as if it was personal. "You've been screwing Susie's sister Jerry… and now Susie's going to screw you… her words… not mine."

Jerry Thompson looked like he'd been felled with an axe. If he'd been standing when Franks had delivered his last comment he'd have probably fallen over. But still… he rocked precariously in his chair.

"Once again Inspector." Jerry whispered. "I have no idea what you're talking about?"

"Oh… I think you have." Franks insisted. "In fact… we all know what you've been doing. You're an arrogant bastard aren't you Jerry… you probably thought you'd get away with it?"

"With what…?" Screamed Jerry.

"White Coppice is lovely isn't it?" Franks continued. "Its so peaceful and quiet. I do understand why you decided to buy that cottage Jerry, although I can't imagine much happening there from day to day…nothing unusual anyway.

Unless of course a young woman comes running up your garden path one day, you let her in and give her a good shagging when the wife's at work. And whilst you're doing it she screams her fucking head off so as all the neighbors can hear. Now that's something you would remember isn't Jerry… you and the neighbors?"

The D.I. wasn't really expecting any reply to his last few comments and he didn't get any. And noticeably if Jerry Thompson had slipped any further down in the chair he would literally be on the floor but before that happened Franks wanted to say a few more things.

"So Jerry…" Said the Inspector. "Lets get back to the matter of your very expensive car."

All Jerry could manage was a feint nod of the head.

"We've had a good nosy." Franks smiled. "…We took away a few things… just to have a closer look and see what was what. And everything seemed okay…until… we found this?"

Suddenly Franks conjured up a small clear plastic bag and held it between outstretched finger and thumb and waved it in Jerry's direction. It was sealed at the top but the contents were not hard to see and as Jerry leaned forward instinctively he knew exactly what was in there, it was a very distinctive fluorescent green hair bobble.

"Yeah…" Said Franks triumphantly. "Its one of Sally's hair bobbles. And we know it's definitely hers… because it still has some of Sally's hair wrapped around it… and can you believe it Jerry… we found that in your car?"

"Rubbish…!" Shouted Jerry. "No you didn't Inspector… you didn't find that in my car… never!"

Franks waited patiently for Jerry's protestations to subside but the minute they did he was in there like a shot.

"We did Jerry… trust me." He said emphatically. "You can say whatever you like but it won't change anything. It was on the floor behind the drivers seat. My lads do exactly what they're told, they report back to me directly and they tell it as it is. Our only objective is to get to the truth and find out what's happened to Sally Fraser. So… if you need to tell me something… you better tell me now!"

"I've got nothing to say." Jerry mumbled under his breath. "Absolutely nothing!"

"And Maggie Sutcliffe?" Franks snapped. "What about her… where is she Jerry… can you remember?"

Chapter 19

Tom Smith had looked like shit even before D.I. Franks brought him to the police station and so a day later it was hardly surprising that he smelled as bad as he did. But when the Inspector resumed the interview he noticed straight away that despite the guy's obvious physical appearance, Tom was a lot more communicative and eager to help than he had been previously.

He might look like crap but at least now he wasn't under the influence.

"Are you feeling any better lad?" Franks asked nicely.

"I'm tired Inspector." Said Tom wearily. "But not as dizzy."

"Do you remember anything else... about Sally?" Asked the D.I. "...It's important Tom... really important."

"I know... I know." Said Tom desperately. "And I want you to find her... but it's all mixed up... in my head. I'm not sure what's real any more."

"Okay..." Said Franks. "Now listen... just take a deep breath and try to relax then slowly put your mind back to the very last time you saw Sally. Was she sad or happy? Was she crying? Was she running? What was she doing Tom… do you remember?"

Once again Tom looked pretty vacant. His eyes were wide open and the lights were definitely on but as far as Inspector Franks could determine… unfortunately… there was no one at home.

It was a shame… the guy seemed genuinely as if he wanted to help but he couldn't.

Then all of a sudden miraculously the guy began to talk. What he said was more of a mumble at first and hardly recognizable but as he continued somehow the words began to make sense.

"Susie thinks I drugged her?" Said Tom.

"Susie…?" Said Franks. "I don't understand… why would she think that?"

"I don't know." Said Tom anxiously. "But that's what Sally told me."

"When…?" Asked the D.I. "When did Sally tell you that?"

"On Saturday…" Insisted Tom. "The night she came over."

"And what did you say?"

"I told her that I wouldn't do that." Said Tom. "Never…"

"And did she believe you?"

"Yeah… she did." Said Tom confidently. "I told her that I'd never do that to Susie… because I loved her."

"And do you love Susie…Tom?" Said Franks. "Do you…?"

"I've always loved her." Said Tom.

"So what did Sally say when you told her that?" Asked the Inspector.

"She said she believed me… because she knew what really happened." Said Tom.

"And what did really happen to Susie?" Asked the D.I. "Did Sally say?"

"Yeah…" Insisted Tom. "Sally told me everything."

"And what was that…?" Argued Franks.

"That it was her… it was Sally!" Said Tom. "It was Sally that drugged her."

"Sally…?" Franks announced. "… Are you sure?"

"Definitely." Tom confirmed.

"And why would she do that?" Asked the Inspector.

"I don't know?" Said Tom. "… I think she hated her."

"And how did that make you feel?"

"I don't know what you mean?" Said Tom suspiciously.

"When you found out that Sally had drugged Susie…" Insisted Franks. "Did it make you angry?"

"Angry…?" Murmured Tom. "… No… it didn't make me angry… why would it?"

"Well… you've just told me that you love Susie." Said Franks. "And then you find out that someone's drugged her… it must have made you feel something."

"Pity… that's all." Said Tom. "It's a shame they couldn't get on… I mean… for Christ's sake… they were sisters. They should have sorted out their differences a long time ago… it's bloody stupid if you ask me?"

"So it didn't make you want to hurt Sally?" Said the Inspector tauntingly. "You know… teach her a lesson for what she'd done?"

"No…" Said Tom loudly. "No it didn't… it never crossed my mind."

"So why did you say… were?"

"I don't know what you mean?" Tom grimaced.

"You said… were sisters…?" Franks insisted.

"No I didn't!" Shouted Tom.

"Yes you did." Said the Inspector. "Were sisters… that's exactly what you said Tom… I think what you meant to say was… are sisters… slip of the tongue eh… maybe?"

"Go to hell…" Tom screamed suddenly. "You can all go to fucking hell… That's it…I'm not saying another word to you bastards… I want a lawyer!"

At that very same moment the door to the interview room opened wide and the sergeant from the front desk slipped in and made his way deliberately towards Franks.

"I need a word boss." He whispered in the Inspector's ear. "I reckon it's important."

The D.I. got to his feet and stepped outside.

"This better be good." He said threateningly. "…Or else."

"It's the kids old fella…" Said the sergeant. "He's at the desk right now… just got back from Spain apparently… and he's doing his nut."

Frank's eyebrows twitched knowingly as he swept away the long black locks of hair that loitered menacingly across his puffy arrogant face. He knew Fred Smith was due back from his latest vacation over the next few days but was hoping that it wouldn't be quite so soon.

"Yeah…" The sergeant continued. "He wants to see his son… immediately. And if he doesn't… he's threatening to call the Chief Constable. Oh yeah… and he wants to know why there's a bunch of hairy-arsed coppers turning his farmhouse upside down and said god help us if we haven't got a warrant?"

"Chief Constable eh…?' Said the D.I. "He'll have a job getting hold of him… he's on holiday… he's in France."

"So… what shall I say boss?" Asked the sergeant.

"Just tell him I'm very busy at the moment." Insisted Franks. "But if he wants to wait… I'll speak to him as soon as I can."

"Okay boss." Said the sergeant. "I'll go and speak to him."

"Oh… and sergeant?" Franks growled. "…Come back and tell me what he says."

"Yeah…" The sergeant smiled. "Will do."

The D.I. was at a crucial point in the investigations and he'd no intention of releasing anyone at this stage. He believed that before the day was out he would be in a position to charge at least one of the guys he had in custody. He had three likely candidates in the station and intended to bring charges against one or more of them for either abduction or possibly kidnapping. It was a serious accusation and one that Franks would not make lightly. All he required was a little more time and what he didn't need was any interference.

The D.I. grabbed a quick sandwich and a coffee in the police canteen then trudged slowly along the corridor until he came to the toilets. He was desperate for a pee anyway but the longer he left the suspects alone to think things over, the more likely it was, he'd get one of the poor sods to crack and tell him everything. He was an expert when it came to interviews and with so many previous scalps already under his belt, he felt confident that he could secure a confession. Franks hadn't made Inspector playing by the rules, and as far as he was concerned the job was a war of attrition and actually there were no rules.

He'd barely had time to zip his flies up however when the sergeant from the front desk burst into the bogs to find him.

"For Christ's sake man..." Shouted Franks. "... Is nothing sacred anymore...? What do you want?"

"Sorry boss..." Insisted the young cop. "...But you said to let you know... what Fred Smith was going to do?"

"Yeah...yeah..." Snarled the Inspector. "Go on... tell me."

"Well the thing is boss... I don't know?"

"What do you mean?" Snapped Franks. "What did he say... how did he react?"

"He just listened..." Said the sergeant. "Very... very quietly... and then he just turned around and walked out of the station... never said another word... and that was it?"

Franks stared at the sergeant puzzlingly... shrugged his shoulders then brushed past the man and made his way back onto the corridor heading in the direction of

Tom Smith. The D.I. was just about to re-enter the interview room when he heard someone else call out his name yet again and instinctively… Franks knew it was trouble.

"Please… hang on boss?" It was PC Fairclough. "You've got an in-coming phone call Sir… it's the Chief Constable."

"Can't be…?" Said Franks.

"No…it is Sir." Said the young bobby emphatically. "He insists I find you and put you on the line immediately… says he's got to speak with you… and it's urgent!"

"He's in France… on his holidays… for God's sake." Insisted the Inspector. "… Are you sure its him?"

"Oh… yeah!" Said the PC. "He's in Paris… its him alright Sir… definitely!"

"Right." Said Franks emitting a long deep audible breath. "I'll take it… okay. Put it through to the back office, I need some privacy."

"Yes Sir…" Said PC Fairclough. "…Right away."

The Inspector sat down and composed himself before lifting the receiver. He knew damned well who was behind all this but despite his anger and frustrations he'd have to listen carefully, his reputation and maybe his job even depended on what might happen in the next few minutes and then of course… there was also his promotion prospects to consider.

"Hello Chief Constable." Said Franks confidently. "…I trust that you're having a good holiday over there in Gay Paree?"

"I was…" Snapped the big chief. "Until now… But lets cut out all the crap shall we Franks… and get straight to the point."

"If you say so." Said Franks quietly.

"Yeah I do…" Insisted the chief. "So… why have you arrested Fred Smith's lad… what exactly has he done?"

"That's still to be determined." Franks sounded cautious. "… And just to clarify the situation Sir… Tom Smith is not under arrest… he's just helping us with our enquiries."

"Bollocks!" Said the chief. "That's not what it sounds like?"

"And… he's not been charged with anything." Insisted Franks. "…Not yet?"

"And he's not going to be." Said the chief angrily. "… Do you hear me?"

"Oh yeah… I hear you Sir." Said the Inspector. "… But with the greatest respect… I don't understand how you can say that. I'm here at the scene with all the information and you're five hundred miles away in Paris with no knowledge of what's going on?"

"Don't get smart with me Franks." Shouted the chief. "I know what's going on… and its going to stop… right now?"

"We have two young girls missing Sir." Said the Inspector loudly. "They've been missing for days… I suspect foul play."

"Listen to me carefully Inspector Franks." Insisted the big boss. "Young girls go missing all the time… it's a fact. Then usually a few days later they turn up again… all fit and well. And we all wonder what all the fuss was about… am I right?"

"Yeah… you're right." Admitted Franks. "But this Sir… this is different."

"Nonsense…!" Snapped the Chief Constable. "You're over-reacting man, get a grip."

"Excuse me?" Said Franks.

"You heard me." Said the chief. "Fred Smith is a close personal friend of mine, him and Mavis. I've known them for years. I'll vouch for him and his son… there's no problem. So what I expect you to do straight away man, immediately I put the phone down, I want you to release the lad… let him go. He's done nothing… I guarantee it. Yeah he's a bit odd, I'll give you that… but he's harmless enough."

"And if I don't Sir…?" Said Franks bluntly. "What then?"

"Oh you will..." Insisted the chief. "Or you can say goodbye to that pension of yours... it must be worth quite a bit by now...eh?"

"And is there anything else you want to say Sir?" Whispered the Inspector.

"Oh yeah there is one other thing..." Insisted the chief. "Get our lads off Fred Smith's property straight away. And if you do it quickly... he's promised not to bring any action against the force... you get me?"

"Loud and clear Sir." Said Inspector Franks. "... In fact...it couldn't be clearer!"

"Good man." Snapped the Chief Constable. "I knew we could count on you... Oh and by the way...there is a vacancy for Superintendent coming up soon... we'll discuss it as soon as I get back... okay?"

"Yes... of course." Said Franks. "... Thank you Sir!"

K. E. Heaton

Chapter 20

Losing his key witness in the case of the two missing girls was a big disappointment to D.I. Franks but when within a few hours of releasing Tom Smith he had a visit from two senior coppers from the Cumbria police force he realized immediately that unless the young women returned of their own accord… they might never be found.

There'd been a lot of huge robberies in the sixties and seventies both in the U.K. and abroad but nothing compared to what had happened in Lebanon in January earlier that year.

On the 20th of January 1976 a group associated with Yasser Arafat's Palestine Liberation Organization exploited the chaos of the country's civil war and broke into the British Bank of the Middle East in Beirut. They used brute force to blast through the bank wall that was shared with a Catholic Church and with the help of a number of foreign mercenaries the gang then cracked the bank's vault and plundered its contents. The loot included up to £50 million pounds worth of gold bars, millions of pounds in foreign currencies and a shed load of jewelry.

Every police force in the world was on the look out for stolen goods connected to the robbery and likewise for any possible participants. There was a strong belief that only former members of the British SAS could have carried out the raid with such thoroughness and expertise.

What the two policemen from Cumbria wanted to do was interview both Bob Fraser and his son-in-law Jerry Thompson at the earliest opportunity. Not concerning any missing girls but in regard to a clandestine meeting that had taken place the previous weekend in the Lake District between a number of hardened criminals and ex soldiers when they'd been recorded discussing the Lebanese raid and the Bank of America robbery in 1975. The police already had mug shots of the two Lancashire men both of whom had been identified by local Cumbrian residents and it soon become blatantly obvious to Inspector Franks that both Fraser and Thompson, slippery as they were, were most unlikely to be involved in either of the girl's sudden disappearance.

Despite what the D.I. may have been considering the two men could not have been in two separate places at the same time and therefore in less than an hour, the number of possible kidnappers had been reduced to zero.

By Thursday evening photographs of the two girls had been printed in both local newspapers and in many of the national rags. North West stations had covered the story each night on television but still despite the coverage five days later there was still no news. Large groups of civilians advised by the emergency services were up on the moors searching for the lasses but apart from random finds of clothing and suspect bones being found there was little to report. None of the clothing found had any connection to either girl and each time the experts were called in to examine the bones, it was always the same... they had numerous bits of sheep, cows and even horses but not once were human remains ever discovered.

Two weeks later worryingly... the trail was getting cold.

With Bob Fraser and Jerry Thompson out of the way, held on remand in Dumfries, at least Susie and Pat could try and get on with their lives as best they could, without any hassle from their respective partners. The fact that both men were banged up awaiting trial was a godsend and the search for Sally went on unhindered by any unwanted interference by either man. As the weeks went by however reports of sightings of the girls diminished considerably, it was a worrying indication that people were losing interest but it did mean that both women especially Pat were not living their lives continually on the edge subject to a see-saw of emotions every time a new report came in.

In a few weeks time it would be Christmas and then in early spring Susie was due to give birth. The police had obviously scaled down their search operations despite their assurances to the contrary, Sally Fraser and Maggie Sutcliffe were both still missing... but life was most definitely moving on.

When word got round that Tom Smith had been interviewed by the police in regard to the girl's disappearance, a number of newspaper photographers camped outside Fred's property for a few days trying to get pictures of him but as typical December weather kicked in they were never going to stay very long. The West Pennine moors could be beautiful in the summer but in winter conditions could be harsh with high winds and lashing rain and with no shelter apart from their vehicles, they soon packed up and headed back to town.

And then two days before Christmas Harry Sutcliffe was found dead in his car one morning outside his own house presumably he'd been there all night and although the police were initially quite suspicious a post mortem proved conclusively that the guy had suffered a massive heart attack and foul play was eventually ruled out. The stress of Maggie's disappearance may well have contributed to Harry's already poor health but after a lifetime of heavy drinking and womanizing his early demise was always on the cards. Instinctively Inspector Franks arranged a special meeting with the press to try and encourage them to give as much coverage as they could to Harry's untimely death in order that if Maggie was in hiding somewhere and free to do what she wished, and she learned that her father had died, it might encourage her to return and attend his funeral. The press agreed to help and because nothing could be arranged at church until the third week of January due to the holidays, there was plenty of time to get the word out there. But... when the burial took place on Tuesday the eighteenth of January, nineteen seventy-seven, the service was poorly attended and needless to say Maggie never showed up.

She's Missing

A cold North Westerly weather pattern hit the U.K. that week and bitter winds brought plummeting temperatures accompanied by rain, sleet and snow. As the icy conditions continued and moved further South down the country it brought even more blizzards and yet deeper snow. And so in the depths of another Lancashire winter despite the efforts of many still desperate to find the two missing girls the trail wasn't just cold... it was positively frozen.

It was only in April when the snows had thawed that Pat Fraser had something to celebrate. She'd lost a daughter the previous year and even though her relationship with Sally had always been turbulent she had missed the girl terribly. In fact with neither Sally nor Bob to fight with life may have become more settled and predictable but it was tedious. Apart from her weekly visits from Susie and Billy Marsden who she could now entertain at the house these days, something he could never have done when Bob was around, Pat's life had become quite monotonous.

And so the patter of tiny feet soon changed all that and when Susie gave birth to a beautiful baby boy weighing in at eight and a half pounds, Pat suddenly had new purpose.

It was apparent to Susie's mum however that something wasn't quite as it should be. Yes... Susie was gorgeous so it stood to reason that she'd have good-looking children but this kid looked nothing like Jerry. Pat's new grandson had a mass of dark black hair, unruly and disobedient just like his mothers and absolutely none of Jerry characteristics. Jerry

Thompson with his warm reddish blonde hair, pale skin and sticky out eyes had been at the back of the queue when they'd given out the handsome genes but his son had grabbed a bag full.

In the weeks running up to the birth Susie had worked tirelessly to put in place everything that would be needed to keep Gladrights on an even keel whilst she was away from the office. She'd been very adept at handling the situation when it became obvious that Jerry wasn't coming back, at least not in the foreseeable future and if everything went to plan she and her new son could live the life she wanted free of interference from either Jerry Thompson or her father.

"He's beautiful…" Insisted Pat. "… Absolutely beautiful."

"Thanks mum." Susie smiled. "…I'm so happy… honestly."

"Good." Pat laughed. "I'm glad… but I never asked you… did I… about names?"

"No… you didn't." Susie frowned slightly. "Although really… there is only one name I could chose."

"Yeah…?" Said Pat curiously.

"Yeah…" Insisted Susie. "…Its William… but you and me mum… we can call him Billy… would you like that?"

"I would like that." Said Pat tearfully. "Yeah… I would… in fact I'd love that… you're a good girl Susie… you always were."

Chapter 21

Following on from the U.K.'s previous years high temperatures and endless sunshine, the summer of nineteen seventy seven was pretty much business as usual. It was dull and wet for most of July and August and sales of umbrellas were back to normal. A year on there was still no news about either Sally Fraser or Maggie Sutcliffe and it looked very much as if the police had drawn a blank.

Inspector Franks now a newly promoted Superintendent was back in Manchester working on yet another new investigation and even though the enquiry into the two missing Lancashire girls had not been closed it was in effect considered by many in the force to be a "cold case."

By October a lot of policemen in the North of England were searching frantically for a madman who over recent months had killed a number of young women in Yorkshire but most recently in Manchester. There was no indication that either of the girls from Chorley was a victim of who the police and press alike had now named the "Yorkshire Ripper" but it was something else to consider.

In November Bob Fraser was sentenced to fourteen years imprisonment for his part in numerous crimes both in the U.K. and on the continent but more worryingly for him was the possibility that even after he'd done his time he might still then be extradited to the U.S. to stand trial for additional misdemeanors.

Jerry Thompson received a lesser sentence of ten years and along with his fellow criminal both men were sent directly to Durham jail.

Twelve months on from Harry Sutcliffe's demise and another death occurred that would subsequently change Pat's life yet again. She hadn't seen Billy Marsden for a number of weeks as he helped to nurse his wife after a bad fall but then suddenly Billy turned up one afternoon to announce that she'd died that same morning. He was devastated… they all were.

And the following year completely out of the blue just two days prior to little Billy's birthday a bright red shiny car pulled up outside the cottage in White Coppice. At first Susie hadn't recognized who the caller was but the minute she opened her front door she knew something was afoot.

It was a well-dressed lady aged most likely in her late fifties who Susie could now identify but had never spoken to previously. She'd seen her in town on numerous occasions rushing around with bits of shopping, always impatient and in a hurry, and evidently someone who was "not" as local people would say "short of a bob or two."

The woman had the face of an angel but as Susie would soon learn she also had a core of iron and despite her pained expression would do anything to get what she wanted.

It was Mavis…Tom Smith's mother.

"Susie…?" She smiled awkwardly. "Please…is it possible… could I come in?"

Susie hesitated caught completely unawares and it was only when the youngster toddled towards her from behind and grabbed her leg that she broke her silence. Susie picked up the child immediately with both arms and stepped back inside the house.

"Why not...?" Said Susie. "Come on Billy… say hello… we've got a visitor."

"So…" Said Mavis opportunely as she followed them quickly into the hallway. "…This is Billy… well I can't believe it… what a big boy you are?"

"Yeah…" Said Susie. "He's only one and I can hardly keep up with him."

"They grow up so fast…" Insisted Mavis as she bent over to stroke the lads long black unruly mop of hair.

"That's true." Susie agreed. "So… Missus Smith…what can I do for you?"

"You know who I am then…?" Said Mavis trying to sound surprised.

"I'd be a fool if I didn't…" Said Susie. "… And if there's one thing I'm not… it's a fool… not any more."

"I doubt you ever were...?" Mavis insisted. "As far as I understand it you're a very successful young lady... and a very pretty one at that... if you don't mind me saying."

"Okay..." Insisted Susie. "So... why have you come?"

"Can I be blunt?" Said Mavis.

"Yes!" Snapped Susie. "Say what you want... just get on with it."

"You had a relationship with my son." Mavis argued. "... Am I right?"

Suddenly Susie's face flushed with color and she pulled the child towards her and held him even tighter.

"A relationship?" Said Susie angrily. "... It was hardly that... believe me. Unless of course you consider that me spending one lousy weekend up on the moors with your weirdo son constitutes a relationship... no... trust me! I was never in a relationship with Tom."

Mavis smiled undeterred. "Can I show you a photograph?" She asked.

Susie shook her head. "No... no you can't..." She said. "In fact... I think you better leave."

"Please...!" Insisted Mavis. "...Its important."

Before Susie had time to say another word an eight by six inch color photograph was thrust into her hand with such persistence that it was difficult to ignore. She pretended not to look at it but the little smiley face staring back at Susie just grabbed her attention.

"Who is this…?" Demanded Susie. "…It looks like Billy?"

"Yeah…" Insisted Mavis. "…It does!"

"So… who is it?" Gasped Susie.

"It's Tom…" Said Mavis. "… On his first birthday."

"Rubbish!" Shouted Susie. "… That's not Tom."

"I'm afraid it is." Said Mavis very calmly. "… Its uncanny isn't it?"

"Uncanny…?" Said Susie angrily. "What's that supposed to mean?"

"… Well…if you didn't know any different." Insisted Mavis. "You'd bet that was little Billy here… wouldn't you. But let's face it Susie… we both know why I'm here?"

"No… no I don't." Susie growled. "… So…why don't you just say what's on your mind?"

"My grandson!" Said Mavis. "… I came here to see my grandson!"

"I've not got a clue what you're talking about." Susie laughed awkwardly. "Like I said… it's time for you to leave."

"If you want me to go… I will." Said Mavis. "But first of all…please… just hear me out."

"Let me guess...?" Said Susie. "You want us all to have a blood test... is that right?"

"No..." Insisted Mavis. "That's not what I came for. Like I said before... I just wanted to see my little grandson here... that's all. I don't need a blood test to tell me who Billy's father is... I already know. Its as clear as the nose on your face!"

"You reckon... do you?" Susie giggled nervously.

"Yeah..." Said Mavis. "Its so obvious."

"And how about Tom?" Susie snarled. "If you're all so sure that he's Billy's father... why has he not dared to show his face... has he put you up to this Mavis... has he?"

"No..." Mavis sighed. "No... he's not... I assure you. He's in Australia if you must know... and as far as I can see he's not coming back."

"Australia...?"

"Yeah." Said Mavis. "He's in Brisbane with his uncle. After everything that's happened and all the accusations about your sister... he decided to leave... its probably for the best."

"Oh... I see." Said Susie sharply. "So even though Tom believes that he might have fathered a child... he's still scarpered off at the first opportunity with no intentions of honoring his parental duties or paying his dues... am I right?"

"If its money you need…?" Insisted Mavis. "…You only need to ask?"

"NO…!" Screamed Susie. "I don't need your lousy money… I've got plenty of my own… and I promise you… this child will want for nothing!"

"I was sure you'd say that." Said Mavis as she grasped Susie by the hand. "I know what a good mother you are… and I know that you'll look after him… I just want to be part of his life… and your life as well. That goes for both Fred and me. We'll probably never have another chance… not now… now that Tom's on the other side of the world. Please… Susie?" Mavis pleaded. "Please… let us see little Billy now and again… I beg you?"

"I don't know… I just don't know." Said Susie shaking her head from side to side her eyes darting back and forth towards the child. "We'll have to see…"

"That's all I can ask." Said Mavis offering a feint smile. "But just imagine… in a few years time this little boy will be very rich. He'll inherit everything… we've no-one else to leave it to Susie… he's our only grandchild and the only one we're ever likely to get…. Please… think about it?"

K. E. Heaton

Chapter 22

It was nineteen eighty-three and the summer was almost at an end. Pat Fraser had just finished the dishes and was looking to put her feet up for an hour but a heavy knock on the front window put paid to that.

When Pat opened the door she was more than surprised, and if there was one person she hadn't seen for some time it was Sergeant Bradshaw.

"Hello Pat." The sergeant mumbled quietly. "…Is it convenient…can I come in please?"

"Of course." Said Pat somewhat anxiously. "…You're always welcome here sergeant… you know that."

As the policeman stepped inside Pat's blood pressure hit the roof. Seldom did any of the Chorley police call in to see her these days and when they did… it was never good news.

"Go on Sam…" Pat insisted immediately. "Spill it out…you didn't come here to talk about the weather."

"No I didn't… you're right." The sergeant agreed. "But when I heard the news… I decided to come and see you straight away."

"It's Sally isn't it…?" Pat sat down instinctively as the color drained from her face.

"No…no… don't fret." Sam Bradshaw had obviously underestimated the impact his sudden intrusion might cause. "It's not Sally…" He stressed. "It's Bob… there's been an incident at Durham jail… he's in hospital."

"What…?" She asked. "Why… what's happened?"

"He got in a fight… apparently." The sergeant continued. "With another inmate. Bob was stabbed in the neck… it's not good I'm afraid."

"When?" Pat mumbled. "…When was this?"

"Last week… some time." Said sergeant Bradshaw. "They operated the same day and it looked like he was over the worst but in the last couple of days he's deteriorated."

"How do you mean?" Said Pat.

"Well… as far as I understand it…" Bradshaw insisted. "He's developed septicemia… and according to the doctors it looks unlikely that he'll pull through."

"So… what now?" Said Pat tentatively.

"He wants to see you Pat." Said the sergeant. "He's asked to speak with you?"

"No…" Pat growled. "I won't… I don't want to see him… ever… ever again."

"Are you sure?" Asked the cop. "...It might be important?"

"There's nothing... absolutely nothing." Insisted Pat. "... That I've got to say to that...to that... man."

"I understand." Said the sergeant as he placed his hands reassuringly on Pat's shoulders. "But... I have to tell you Pat... he has mentioned Sally... Bob insists he's got something really important to tell you... and he refuses to speak to anyone else... anyone apart from you?"

"I can't Sam." Said Pat. "...I just can't... you must understand?"

"I do understand love... believe me." Stressed the sergeant. "... But you must realize... if you don't go Pat... you're never going to find out what he wanted to tell you... please... just think about it."

At first light they headed north up the M6 towards Durham. The sergeant reckoned on two and a half hours to cover the one hundred and twenty miles to Her Majesty's category A prison which first opened its doors to some of the UK's worst offenders in 1819 and it wasn't just men that gave this particular establishment its notorious reputation.

Between 1869 and 1958 a total of ninety-five inmates ended their days hanging by the neck from the gallows at Durham Jail and a number of them were women.

Bob Fraser wouldn't finish his days on the end of a rope but when he did take his final breath Pat would be right there beside him… hanging on to Bob's every last word.

When Pat first walked into the prison infirmary with sergeant Bradshaw it filled her full of dread. She'd sworn to herself all those years ago when Bob was arrested that she would never speak to the man again but now she'd decided this was something she simply had to do. As Sam Bradshaw had rightly said if she didn't find out what Bob wanted to say to her, he'd take whatever information he might have about Sally… to the grave.

"Hello Pat." Bob whispered. "… Long time no see."

"Yeah…" Said Pat. "…It's been a while."

"But now you've come…" Bob's voice was even more feint. "… I knew you would."

"Oh yeah…" Said Pat defensively. "…Why's that that?"

"Because…" Bob mumbled. "… You need to know… don't you Pat… what went on?"

"And what did go on Bob?" Said Pat. "… Tell me?"

"I won't tell you anything." Bob insisted as he pointed feebly towards the sergeant. "…Until… he leaves us alone."

Pat turned her head instinctively towards Sam Bradshaw. She didn't want the sergeant to leave her alone with the monster… god knows she'd been in that position too many times before… but if Bob insisted… what could they do?

"Don't worry Pat." Said the sergeant. "I'll go… but if you want me… I'm right outside… okay?"

"Okay…" Pat agreed.

"Yeah… that's right." Whispered Bob. "… Just do as you're told copper… and fuck off."

Sam Bradshaw smiled as he stepped away from the bed… Bob Fraser's comments meant nothing to him. He could only feel contempt for the man and like all good policemen… he'd heard it all before.

"Well… what is it Bob?" Asked Pat. "… That you've dragged me all the way up here to tell me?"

"…You're a hard woman Pat Fraser." Insisted Bob. "… You weren't always like this… remember?"

"Oh I remember all right." Said Pat loudly. "I remember everything… every put down, every threat every slap in the face… how could I forget?"

"Really…" Said Bob quietly. "… Was it actually that bad?"

"No…" Said Pat. 'It was ten times worse than that… and you know it."

"I'm sorry." Bob croaked suddenly. "Please… believe me… I'm so sorry."

215

"Then for once in your life just do the right thing… tell me… you bastard." Said Pat angrily. "…Just tell me what you know… and then I can leave?"

Bob gulped. He had two choices. If he'd thought for a minute that Pat would beg him to tell her what he knew… then he was obviously mistaken and if he chose to die in silence then he'd achieved absolutely nothing… and so reluctantly he began to talk.

"That big row I had…" Bob whispered. "With Sal… before she went missing."

"Yeah… what about it?" Said Pat.

"I knew then that something was going on." Bob insisted. "…That's why I confronted her."

"You were always confronting people Bob." Said Pat her voice still trembling with anger. "It's what you've always done… that's exactly why you're here now."

"No… listen to me." Bob's words were getting fainter with every effort. "You see a few days before we argued… I saw her… Sally… I saw her with someone."

Instinctively Pat moved closer. "Who was it… who was it Bob?"

Bob Fraser was trying hard to keep it all together but the truth was his body was spiraling rapidly out of control. He was feverish, his blood pressure had begun to drop and his heart rate was abnormally high. He was in mortal danger and when his body succumbed eventually to what the experts called septic shock he would lose conscientious completely for the very last time and he would die.

"I had lots of other women Pat." Bob whispered. "...Lots!"

"I know..." Said Pat. "... So what?"

"That other girl... the one that went missing." Bob mumbled. "I went with her too."

"Maggie Sutcliffe...?" Said Pat loudly. "...You had it off with her?"

"Yeah..." Said Bob. "... Maggie... she was lovely."

"And what has she got to do with all this Bob?" Said Pat. "...Tell me... now."

"Maggie dumped me..." Bob suddenly announced. "And then I saw her... that night... in town."

"Where...?" Said Pat. "...Where in town?"

"At Gladrights." Said Bob a little more animated.

"With Jerry...?" Said Pat.

"Yeah... with Jerry." Bob agreed. "... Susie's better off without him."

"Yeah... Susie knows that." Said Pat. "... So what did you do Bob?"

"Well...when Maggie left Gladrights." Said Bob. "...I followed her... into town. I was going to have a word with her… find out what the hell she was playing at?"

"And did you…?" Asked Pat strenuously.

"No…" Said Bob quietly. "I couldn't… could I?"

"Why Bob?" Said Pat. "Why couldn't you?"

"Because it was then." Said Bob. "… She met Sally!"

"Are you sure?" Snapped Pat. '… Are you sure it was Sally?"

"Oh yeah… it was our Sally alright." Bob insisted. "…No doubt about it."

"So…?" Said Pat defensively. "…What does that prove?"

"I watched them…" Said Bob. "I watched them for ages… in fact I couldn't stop myself… I just couldn't believe it?"

"What…?" Pat begged. "What were they doing…?"

"Well… put it this way." Bob insisted. "…It wasn't right."

"Oh… for God's sake man." Pat screamed. "…Just tell me will you."

"They were all over each other…" He stressed. "They were snogging each others face off… I tell you… and not just that… they were messing with each other as well... if I hadn't seen it with my own eyes... I tell you Pat... I would never have believed it."

Pat fell silent. She didn't know what to say. Bob was a wicked man and he'd done some horrible things but for the first time ever, she did believe him... and not only that... she was glad.

"Do you want to know what I think Pat...?" Said Bob his voice increasingly feint.

"Yeah... yeah I do." Said Pat. "...Tell me?"

"I think she's still alive..." Said Bob tears streaming down his face. "... I've always thought it."

"Me too..." Said Pat. "...Yeah... me too!"

Bob died later that night as Pat prepared to head back to Lancashire. And when Pat phoned Susie a little later to let her know the news... neither woman shed a tear. Sally's biological dad may have passed away but Susie's father was still alive and kicking. All Susie needed now was a way to get rid of Jerry... and when she had... her future with little Billy would be secure.

K. E. Heaton

Chapter 23

Susie's willingness to accept Mavis and Fred Smith as her young sons grandparents had been a good move and Fred's influence apparently knew no boundaries.

In the autumn of nineteen eighty-four Jerry Thompson was due for release on parole. If Jerry violated certain conditions then he'd be back inside before he could blink and so when Fred Smith paid him a visit a few weeks before his release date and made him an offer he couldn't refuse it was agreed there and then that Susie and little Billy would never set eyes on the man… ever again.

At the time Susie never asked Fred what had been said… but the truth was… she didn't care. Tom was in Australia Bob was six feet under and now finally… Jerry Thompson was banished. All Susie's adversaries had gone or been made to disappear with little or no possibility of them ever coming back… although there was still one that might return one day… who knows? And that was Sally!

In nineteen ninety-five Pat agreed to marry Billy Marsden the man she's always loved. It was a small affair at Preston Register Office followed by a reception for family members and a few close friends at the Pines Hotel in Clayton-Le-Woods near Chorley. All the children from their previous marriages with the exception of Sally of course attended and everyone appeared genuinely overjoyed that eventually their two surviving parents had tied the knot. Gone were the days when religion decided what was allowed and who could marry whom and at long last it seemed attitudes had changed… common sense had finally prevailed.

There wasn't a day went by however when Susie and Pat in particular didn't think about Sally but in truth both women had never been happier.

Then suddenly one day in late spring nineteen ninety-nine human remains were found on the hills above Chorley. It resulted in many weeks of additional anxiety for all concerned until eventually the findings were identified as male and of middle eastern descent.

Young Billy as Pat always described her very handsome grandchild had begun to make a name for him self. He'd been introduced to Fred's business from an early age and as Fred Smith was moving gradually towards the end of his working life it was generally accepted that Billy would take over the firm and that one-day eventually… as Mavis had promised all those years ago, he'd inherit the lot.

As the years passed Billy's position strengthened. He looked a lot like Tom his father. He had thick black hair combed straight back from a high forehead, noticeably long and hanging down at the back over his shoulders. And in fact just like his dad he'd become the most eligible bachelor in Chorley and the surroundings districts.

It wasn't just Billy's looks though that made him so popular. His confident self-assured manner was a natural attraction. He was softly spoken but when he did speak people listened. He was patient but very determined. Even the men found it hard to resist him and just like Fred… he was a natural leader who commanded respect.

He had of course inherited several other noticeable traits from the Smiths and in particular from his grandfather. When he needed to, Billy could be extremely hardheaded, took his responsibilities very seriously and would never shy away from making difficult decisions.

One evening when Billy was otherwise engaged Susie drove across to see Fred at his place up on the moors. She seldom visited the house, it brought back too many unwanted memories, but when she did he and Mavis always made her feel more than welcome.

"I need a word Fred?" Said Susie as if she meant business. "Please… if I may?"

"I'll leave you to it…" Said Mavis. "… Sounds like work?"

"Yeah…" Said Susie in agreement. "… I suppose it is really."

"Right…" Said Fred. "…Sit down love… what can I do for you?"

Susie made herself comfortable, and if previous chats with Fred were anything to go by, she might be there for a while.

"It's the business…?" Said Susie directly. "… And Billy!"

"Okay." Said Fred. "… But to be fair Susie… it's a big subject and there's a lot to talk about. You'll have to give me a bit more to go on."

"He's very similar to you Fred?" Said Susie. "… And that's not a criticism… believe me… but?"

"But what…?" Fred smiled.

"Look… " Said Susie quite excitedly. "I know you run a very successful business Fred…"

"Yeah I do…!" Fred interjected proudly. "… And one day it'll all be Billys."

"I understand." Said Susie. "…Trust me… I do understand… and Billy and I are both very grateful for that and for everything else that you and Mavis have helped us with over the years."

"So…!" Said Fred. "… Then what's the problem?"

"It's the other business Fred…" Said Susie solemnly. "The other things you do that are not perhaps… dare I say… as legitimate as the ones we see day to day."

"I don't know what you mean love." Said Fred quietly. "Really… I've not got a clue what you're talking about."

"Alright…" Said Susie. "Please… tell me this then… if you will… that day… you went to see Jerry for me… at Durham jail. What did you say to him Fred?"

"Does it matter?" Insisted Fred. "I mean… the main thing was… to make sure he never showed his face here… ever again… and did he?"

"No… he didn't." Susie agreed. "But why… why didn't he just tell you to get lost… and come back anyway… I don't understand?"

"Six figures love…" Said Fred bullishly. "…That's why!"

"What…?" Susie gasped. "… You actually paid him that sort of money just to make sure he stayed away… really?"

"Yeah…" Said Fred. "Yeah I did… because he'd kept his part of the bargain."

"What bargain…?" Asked Susie now desperate to learn more. "You'd made a deal with Jerry… surely not?"

"Oh yeah… we'd made a bargain all right." Fred sighed. "So… I suppose you want to know… do you?"

"Yes I do." Said Susie. "… Definitely."

"Okay…" Said Fred as he pulled himself up in his chair and stared directly at Susie's face. "If you must know… when Jerry and Bob went to jail… we were all part of the same gang… all three of us. I know this is hard to believe love… but its true… all of it. They got caught in a sting operation… that night… up in the Lake District. Only… I wasn't there… was I… and I never got caught?"

"So… you and Bob… and Jerry?" Said Susie. "You're right… I don't believe it."

"Well that's up to you…" Said Fred. "But I may as well carry on and tell you the whole story. I looked after all the loot Susie… well most of it… apart from certain bits that went astray. And they kept quiet those two… they couldn't really do anything else… could they? So then… as you know Bob died… which meant that when Jerry was released he was due his share… plus some… and when I gave it to him… he promised me that he would never return ever… And if he's got any sense… he never will!"

"So… hang on Fred?" Susie insisted. "… This loot… as you put it… were did it all come from… I don't understand?"

Fred sighed.

"What you must understand love." Said Fred. "Is that when things went a bit quiet around here… you know… like they do… when factories close and people are thrown out of work… it happens all the time. The building work dries up and there's no alternative… a man has to find something else to do… to occupy his time. I was asked to do some renovation work… on the rock."

"On the rock…?" Asked Susie with a puzzled look on her face.

"Yeah..." Said Fred. "Gibraltar... so I went over with a few of the lads and who should I meet up with... but Bob... and some of his old army mates?"

"Really...?" Said Susie. "So what was he up to over there?"

"All sorts of stuff." Said Fred. "I never liked the man... but he did introduce me to lots of other guys who I got along with just fine."

"A bunch of crooks... no doubt?" Susie insisted. "I was only a kid... but I can still remember some of the unsavory characters who used to call at the house to see him."

"Well there you go then..." Fred grimaced. "And if I'm honest... I was one of them."

"But what sort of things were you doing Fred... in Gibraltar and elsewhere... can you tell me?"

"Okay..." Fred whispered. "If you must... like everything it started very small... just a bit of smuggling actually... ferrying bits of contraband around the coast... it was mainly from Morocco and into Spain... nothing major. Just pocket money really. That is... until we got organized... and the robberies began."

"Robberies...?"

"Oh yeah dozens of them... we hit all kinds of targets... it was so easy... believe me." Fred insisted. "But then like everything else... it escalated... big time... until eventually... it was the banks."

"Now... I don't believe you..." Said Susie. "Not you Fred... please... tell me you're making all this up?"

"I wish I was love." Fred insisted. "But no... its true... all of it... and I'm not proud... but it happened... and I can't change that... and that's where we are... okay?"

"And Jerry...?" Said Susie sounding even more amazed with every breath. "...When did he get involved?"

"He was a clever guy... with a lot of balls." Said Fred. "He'd obviously heard something on the grapevine and he wanted a piece of the action... and he wasn't afraid of getting his hands dirty... that's for sure. So when he approached us... eventually... we let him in. He was young, plenty of energy... and an extra bit of muscle... its always useful."

"And have you stopped robbing banks Fred?" Asked Susie sarcastically. "Or are you still at it?"

"No love." Fred sighed. "That stopped along time ago... I promise you... after Beirut... that was the big one... I promise!"

"So Billy...?" Said Susie earnestly. "What does he know about all this...? I want him to be safe... Fred... it's important!"

"He's safe..." Said Fred without any hesitation. "He's safer than any of us... and he's smarter too. Between us Susie... you and Pat, me and Mavis...

we've brought him up proper… but he's no mug trust me… and he never will be!"

Susie was speechless.

"Yeah…" Said Fred confidently. "And God help anyone… who gets in his way!

Chapter 24

Late June 2018

On this particular evening strangely it appeared as if the sun had somehow been granted a stay of execution. Denying the close of play until eventually mercifully the fiery beast was smothered and it slipped down behind the horizon leaving behind it a wonderful sky of pinks and orange. And it was then as Susie was just about ready for bed that ex copper John Fairclough pulled up in his car outside the cottage and strolled down the path towards her door.

Billy was away on holiday for a week with a couple of mates so unusually she'd no one to wait up for, and this unexpected caller therefore, especially at this late hour was someone she could well have done without.

She and Billy had lived happily in the cottage for over forty years and as far as she was concerned he had no intention of moving out. He'd had lots of lady friends and on a couple of occasions had come close to getting hitched but just as events were heading in that direction he would call it all off and willingly throw himself back into the job. As far as mother and son relationships go… theirs would take some beating. Susie was devoted to Billy completely. He was the one good thing that had come out of all the nonsense she'd had to endure previously and all that mattered to Susie was Billy's welfare and his on-going survival.

Susie might well have been in her sixtieth year but she looked fantastic. Like Billy she'd dated a few partners over the years and likewise had turned down numerous proposals of marriage, it wasn't that she hated men… but she did find it very hard to trust the opposite sex and after all… why should she?

The guy now standing in her doorway had shown an interest in Susie for several years since his wife's early death in two thousand and nine. They'd known each other long before that and in fact had first set eyes on each other at Chorley Police Station as far back as nineteen seventy six when Sal first went missing. At the time John Fairclough had been a young copper in the old market town and remembered all too well the day that both Maggie Sutcliffe and then subsequently Sally Fraser had disappeared.

He'd spent over thirty years on the force and prior to his early retirement in two thousand and five eventually after all those years he'd made Inspector.

Susie liked the man and she considered him a good friend but for the time being at least… as far as she was concerned…that was how it would remain.

Susie opened the door slowly and popped her head around… and as she did so… she smiled wearily.

"Hello John." Susie whispered. "… It's a bit late."

She's Missing

"Yeah… I'm sorry." Said John apologetically. "… I'm really sorry Susie… please forgive me… but I have some news… I think you should know."

"Okay…" Susie insisted. "You better come in…"

John Fairclough was a good looking man, extremely tall with sharp rugged features, just a few years older than Susie and a man of integrity. Susie invited him to sit down, she was tired but knew very well that John would never have called so late at night if what he had to say… was not important.

"The thing is Susie…" Said the ex copper. "I've been to see someone this evening… and it's someone you know."

"Go on…" Said Susie tentatively.

"Annie Turner!" John Fairclough smiled. "… She was a good friend of Sally's."

"Yeah… yeah." Said Susie impatiently. "…I know who she is… not my favorite person… I must admit."."

"Really…?" Said John. '…I didn't know."

"Well…" Said Susie. "You're right… she was Sally's friend… but never mine. But that's all a long time ago John… so what's she had to say?"

"She sent me a message… this morning." John insisted. "Wanted to give me something… and talk… about Sally!"

"So…!" Said Susie.

"You may not know this…" Said John. "But the woman's very ill… if fact she's dying… and as far as I see… she's not got long."

"Oh right." Susie whispered. "… I didn't know."

"Yeah…" Said John. "Ovarian cancer apparently… she's in the final stages."

"I'm sorry…" Said Susie. "No one deserves that crap."

"No… you're right." Said John. "And that's why I went to see her."

"And…?" Susie asked.

"And… what she had to say." John sighed loudly. "…Is crucial!"

Susie sat upright in her chair, she'd been feeling sleepy but now suddenly… she was wide-awake and listening intently to what John Fairclough was about to say.

"Crucial…?" Susie begged. "…Why?"

"Well Susie…" John explained. "I suggest you take a deep breath… but it looks to me like Sally… and I presume Maggie Sutcliffe also… they're probably still alive… at least they were ten years ago."

"What…" Susie gasped. "What the heck are you talking about?"

She's Missing

"I've got postcards I can show you." John insisted. "Sally sent them... to Annie... there's six of them altogether. They don't say too much about what's going on... just letting Annie know she's all right... and hoping everything's okay with her... just a few scribbles really."

"Oh yeah..." Said Susie in disbelief. "... And no one else knew... really... surely someone else must have seen them and read them when they were delivered... I'm not sure I believe all this John?"

"No... listen." Said John earnestly. "Annie explained all that to me. All the postcards were sent inside plain envelopes and arrived at different times... between nineteen seventy seven and two thousand and eight... here let me show you."

The ex copper pulled a wad of correspondence out of his top pocket and slapped it down on the coffee table for Susie to examine. Susie leaned forward eagerly but then hesitated somewhat and began to finger the documents judiciously as if they were some kind of precious relic.

"Is this all of them...?" Asked Susie suspiciously.

"I believe so..." Said John. "At least... that's what Annie said."

"And why you...?" Asked Susie. "... Of all people?"

"I don't know." Said John. "You'd have to ask Annie Turner that?"

"No… its okay…I don't need to." Said Susie suddenly. "You're a good man John… I trust you… and apparently… so does Annie."

"I did work on the case… when Sally and Maggie first went missing?" John insisted. " I was a young copper back then… but I've got to say…I remember it all… just as clearly as if it were yesterday."

"These postcards…" Said Susie in astonishment. "…Were they all posted in Ireland?"

"Yeah…that's right…" John agreed. "As far as I can see three of them were posted in Dublin itself, two of them in Bray, County Wicklow and the last one from Greystones… further down on the east coast of Ireland."

"Its hard to believe…" Susie insisted. "… And… Annie Turner… she's known about this for the past forty years."

"Were they very close?" Asked John. "… Sally and Annie?"

"As thick as thieves…!" Susie sighed. "In fact… the more I think about it… it doesn't surprise me."

"Really…?" Said John.

"Oh yeah…" Susie smiled. "The two of them were quite inseparable… a pain in the backside actually… they were always in trouble and no matter what Sally got up to… Annie would always stand by her… even if she'd nothing to do with what ever had happened… Annie would still take the blame for Sally!"

"A true friend then…?" Said John.

"Yeah…" Susie sighed again even more emphatically. "… She was always faithful… if that's what you mean. But what you must understand is… Sally was devious. If you let her… she'd wrap you around her little finger… and that's were Annie came in."

"I was tempted to tell Pat…?" Said John suddenly. "… Do you think I should?"

"No…!" Susie insisted. "Please John… don't do that… not yet anyway. It's not fair… we don't want to get mum's hopes up… do we… and then them have them dashed again… like so many times before?"

"No…" Said John. "… You're right… we don't."

"So…" Asked Susie pointedly. "…What do you suggest?"

"I've decided to go over there next week." John insisted. "… To Ireland… I'll take a look round… see if I can find them… it's the least I can do!"

"That's a good idea…" Susie agreed wholeheartedly. "… And if its okay with you John…I'd like to come with you!"

K. E. Heaton

Chapter 25

When John Fairclough called at Susie's cottage again early on Sunday morning the day was already blisteringly hot. In fact the weather over the previous few weeks had been quite amazing and forecasters were predicting another great summer. Who knows said one of them on breakfast television... "This could be the driest, hottest and sunniest summer since records had begun... and possibly... even as hot as nineteen seventy six."

They were driving down to Holyhead on the North Wales coast that morning and planned to catch the ferry across to Dublin shortly after lunch. Annie Turner had passed away in the early hours and when he heard the sad news a few minutes before leaving town the ex-copper felt sure that his decision to drive to Ireland to try and find the two missing women was more than justified. Susie had spoken to her mum the previous day and told her that she and John had decided to have a few days away together but as far as Pat was concerned this had nothing to do with finding Sally. Pat had always suspected that John Fairclough had a thing for Susie, and she was right, but what would never have crossed Pat's mind were the couple's true intentions.

And as for John this journey was something he simply had to do, as soon as he'd left Annie Turner's bedside a few days earlier he'd made his mind up to try and resolve the question… "What did happen to Sally Fraser and Maggie Sutcliffe, all those years ago?"

The other added bonus was the opportunity he'd been given to spend some time with the woman he'd always loved. Susie was the prettiest young woman he'd ever set eyes on and now forty years on she was still gorgeous and the best looking sixty year old he'd ever seen. They'd always got on really well together and if he played his cards right and was given the chance to prove himself their relationship might just develop in the way that he'd always hoped.

Next stop… Dublin!

The ex-policeman wasn't a particularly rich man but he did enjoy a good pension after his many years on the force and since his wife's death he'd inherited a reasonable sum that would help support him in his golden years. And therefore immediately Susie had offered to go with him to Ireland, John had booked two rooms at the Druids Glen Hotel and Golf resort at Newtown Mount Kennedy in County Wicklow. Less than an hours drive from the port it was he considered an excellent base from where they could conduct a search for Sally Fraser and Maggie Sutcliffe. It wasn't too far from Dublin and close to both Bray and Greystones on the coast, the last two locations that Sally had visited before posting her correspondence to Annie Turner.

He wanted to please Susie with his choice of hotel and when finally they reached their destination John was sure that he'd made the right decision.

Nestled in three hundred and sixty acres of beautiful countryside between the Wicklow Mountains and the Irish Sea it was a sanctuary from the heat and the hustle and bustle of everyday life. It had luxurious guestrooms with all the comforts and elegance that one could ever wish for and if John Fairclough's instincts were not mistaken, Susie was undoubtedly impressed.

The following morning however it was down to work. With John's experience and knowledge of how things worked in order to try and locate the two women they drove straight into Bray and visited the local Gardai. The Irish police were more than helpful but with no recent photographs of either Sally or Maggie it was where to start? The cops made a note of every bit of information that Susie and John could give them and suggested lots of other people they could contact including the local newspapers and even a television company that might possibly cover the story. They took copies of each of the postcards Sally had sent back to Annie Turner in the UK over the first thirty years of their absence and filled out all the necessary forms that would be forwarded on to each of the Irish police departments alerting them to the two missing British females.

Next stop was the Civil Registration Office at the Civic Centre on Main Street where they could search for the two women and see whether their names might possibly appear on the electoral register. It meant also they then had access to the general register for births, marriages and deaths, and a record of the latter they both considered quite likely but only because there hadn't been any correspondence in the last ten years… the truth was however… they hadn't got a clue what they might find!

Their search went on for days in particular around the old Victorian seaside town of Bray itself and then subsequently in Greystones where Sally's very last card had been posted. They chatted to lots of residents many of whom had lived in the area for years but by the following Saturday exhausted by their efforts and despite all the media attention and help they'd received from the authorities and from the public they were no nearer to finding either woman. No one recalled ever knowing anyone by the name of Sally Fraser or Maggie Sutcliffe and as they relaxed over dinner back at the hotel the chances of ever finding Susie's long lost sister seemed as hopeless as they'd always been.

And they were both ready to call it a night when the concierge suddenly stopped them as they summoned the lift to go upstairs to bed. There was a man in reception apparently who wanted to speak with them urgently regarding their search.

When they got there it was little guy in an old shiny suit and black boots sparkling with polish. He had yellow-blonde hair that was parted on one side, held perfectly in place with what Susie assumed must be "Brylcreem" the last few strokes of the man's comb still evident, like a field that had just been ploughed, his wavy locks all very neat and orderly. He smiled as they approached him and as they got nearer Susie moved instinctively to one side not wishing to feint from the overwhelming smell of the man's hair cream and what she could only assume was a cheap cologne the guy had obviously used in abundance.

"Good evening to you both…" Said the man cheerfully. "… And how are you?"

"We're both fine." Said John. "…And you?"

"Ah… " Said the man. "… Well… I could be better."

"Oh right…" John smiled. "… Nothing too serious I hope?"

"Nothing… a couple of whiskies wouldn't cure." Said the man hopefully. "…To be sure!"

"Well in that case." Said John. "…We better get you one… come on… lets go to the bar."

Susie hadn't planned on a nightcap but this old chap despite his odd smell and strange demeanor looked like he might just know something. The only difficulty was the question of how many drinks they might have to buy him before he told them what they wanted to know.

"These… these ladies?" Whispered the old guy. "…The ones you're trying to find… tell me…. are they friends of yours?"

"Yeah…" Said John immediately. "Yes they are!"

"Its important isn't it?" Said the Irishman. "...To know who it is you're talking to."

"Exactly..." Said John. "... And I didn't catch your name...?"

"Pat..." Said the man. "... And yours?"

"You can call me John." The ex-cop insisted. "... And this is Susie."

"That's okay then." Said Pat. "So... now we're all acquainted like... shall we have another drink... its awfully warm in here?"

"I'll get you another whisky Pat." John smiled. "... And how about a pint of the black stuff to go with it?"

"You're a man after me own heart." Said Pat cheerfully. "...So you are."

And so two pints of Guinness and three whisky chasers later the man relaxed somewhat and began to talk.

"Now... from what I understand John." Said Pat. "You're looking for two women... one named Sally and one named Maggie... is that right?"

"Correct..." John agreed. "...The youngest of the two ladies is called Sally Fraser... the eldest... Maggie Sutcliffe. Sally will be almost sixty by now... Maggie's a few years older."

"Well... unfortunately." Whispered the Irishman. "... I've got to tell you... I don't know anybody... by either of those names?"

"What...?" Said Susie sounding quite angry. "... I don't understand?"

"Yeah..." John interjected. "... I thought you said you knew the ladies we were looking for?"

"Is that so...?" Said the little old man. "... Well... maybe I do?"

"Really...?" Said John in disbelief. "... You reckon?"

"Yeah... I reckon!" Said Pat looking even more confident by the minute.

"Go on then...!" John insisted. "... So what do you know?"

"I know its cost you a lot of money to stay here..." Said Pat warily. "... A small fortune... I don't doubt?"

"Okay..." Said John. "...How much?"

"Five hundred Euro's..." Said Pat unflinchingly. "...And I'll tell you exactly where they are... so I will."

John Fairclough stared hard at the man. He'd paid out lots of dosh to people like this over the years... it was how the police got most of their information in the eighties and nineties. Sometimes it was the only way... and even though this was John's own money that he was preparing to cough up…if it meant finding Sally… then so be it.

He placed a wad of notes on the table very, very slowly, but purposely and deliberately refused to release his hold on the cash until he got what he wanted.

"Two hundred…" Said the ex-cop refusing to take his eyes off the man. "…And that's it… that's your lot… don't even try to negotiate… just tell us where they are?"

"…Brittas Bay!" Pat announced suddenly. "That's where you'll find them… and you can take my word on that."

John's hand stayed firmly on the table… he'd no intention of paying for scraps. "Where…?" He demanded. "Whereabouts…?"

"It's a lovely house… I'll tell you that." Said the Brylcreem boy. "On the edge of the dunes… nice and secluded… like."

"What's it called…?" Said John angrily. "… Has it got a name this property?"

"To be sure…" Said Pat. "…It most certainly has."

Still…John wouldn't budge… his fist secure on the wad of ten and twenty Euro notes.

"Just tell us…" Susie insisted. "…For god sakes man… Get on with it."

"Meadow Wood…" Pat suddenly announced. "That's it… that's what its called… now I need to get going… it's getting late."

"Not so fast my little friend…" John smiled as he snatched his hand back away from the table seemingly in order to withdraw his offer. "… I need names?" He demanded. "… Names… now!"

"Flynn…!" Shouted the Irishman angrily. "… Sally and Maggie Flynn… their sisters… okay!"

John dropped the cash on the table and sat back with a big smile on his face.

The old guy snatched up the money and finished his drink in the same movement. Got to his feet as quickly as possible and scarpered off back through reception before you could blink.

"Well then…" Susie kissed John on the cheek with a sudden surge of spontaneity. "…You did good." She added. "… Really good… I'm impressed!"

"Lets hope so…" John grinned. "Although I guess we'll find out in the morning!"

K. E. Heaton

Chapter 26

"Meadow Wood..." Said Susie as they drove right by. "...That's it... that's the house!"

"You...you're sure?" John mumbled as he slammed his foot on the car's brakes and came to a complete standstill.

Brittas Bay was simply idyllic. The large detached house they were looking at from the roadway was in a superb coastal position. Sitting pretty on an elevated secluded site and only accessible via a long private driveway. It enjoyed panoramic views of the Irish Sea and overlooked a five-kilometer stretch of powdery sand and adjacent sand dunes.

The area was covered in wonderful ferns and glorious grassland and not only that the beach had EU Blue Flag credentials. It was undoubtedly... a beautiful and secure place to live.

If Sally had managed somehow to buy a property here in such a wonderful location then no one could deny she'd done well for herself, amazingly well. Susie was visibly shocked and as John was all too aware... his new companion was finding it difficult to take it all in.

"Please John…" Said Susie sharply. "Don't stop… not here anyway… let's park up first… and take a look around."

"Okay…" John agreed obediently as he put the car back in gear and moved slowly away. "…I think there's a good spot up ahead… we can see the beach from there."

They pulled over on to a section of high ground at the side of the road offering a perfect photo opportunity for summer visitors with a commanding view over the whole of Brittas Bay. Only a hundred meters or so from the rear of what they understood might well be Sally's property and at long last within striking distance of Susie's long lost sister. Could all this be happening… really…? Susie wasn't quite sure.

But then all of a sudden… Susie could hardly believe it… As her eyes scanned the beach initially they were then drawn subsequently to give further attention to two rather mature ladies sat out on the sands behind the big house… and it was then she recognized immediately her younger sibling… she was forty years older than when she'd last seen her… but there was no doubt in her mind… none whatsoever… the woman she was looking at… was definitely Sally!

"Well… I'll be jiggered." Susie muttered under her breath almost incomprehensibly. "… It's her… it's actually her!"

"Are you sure…?" John gasped. "… Really?"

"I'd know that face anywhere…" Said Susie. "… Trust me!"

"So… what do you want to do…?" Said John eventually. "…Do you know?"

"No…I'm not sure…" Said Susie. "… Please… just let me think."

John sat back and closed his eyes. He was desperate to speak with Sally and to find out where she'd been for the past four decades but ultimately he had to respect Susie's wishes and after all she was Sally's sister.

"I'm going down there…" Susie insisted suddenly. "Straight away… before I change my mind."

"Okay…" Said John. "…I'm with you… let's go."

"Alone…" Susie snapped. "…I'm sorry John… I'm really sorry… it's just that… you've got to understand… this is something I have to do by myself… okay?"

"Okay!" Said John eventually. "… I do understand… I do honestly… but if you need me… just shout."

"I will." Said Susie as she pushed open the car door. "… I promise."

Susie climbed out of the car and hurried down on to the beach and through the dunes. She was hidden from view for a few minutes until eventually she cleared the huge mounds and stepped out onto the hard sand and headed off in the direction of the two women. As Susie got closer to her target she noticed Maggie reach out to touch Sally's hand in order to draw her attention to the arrival of the approaching interloper. Sally looked up slowly and stared across to meet Susie's gaze as she came ever nearer. She had a vacant look in her eye that never faltered and although Susie was sure that Sal had recognized her, the woman remained seated as Susie approached… her sister's face was completely unmoved… refusing to flinch… not even for a second.

"Well…" Said Sally cold-heartedly. "… Would you believe it… it's my big sister… so…well done our kid…you've finally caught up with me… it took you long enough?"

Susie hadn't given it much thought really as to what she might say to Sal if she ever saw her again… but after that… what could she say.

"Cat's got your tongue then… eh?" Sally insisted. "…Come on… don't fool yourself Susie… after all…what did you expect. We couldn't stand each forty years ago… I can't imagine things have changed that much… can you?"

"No… maybe not." Said Susie calmly. "…But I was prepared to try."

"Why…?" Shouted Sal. "…Why bother… its too late?"

"It's never too late…" Susie whispered.

"Oh yeah... trust me." Sally grinned. "It really is too late... anyway... what the hell are you doing here... and how did you find me?"

"Annie Turner..." Said Susie quietly. "...We found out from Annie."

"Annie didn't tell you anything." Sal insisted. "... That's for sure?"

"No she didn't..." Susie agreed. "...But we were given the letters... after she died."

"Oh right..." Sally whispered. "... That's a shame... that's a real shame... but now I understand... so what do you want?"

"I just wanted to see you again." Said Susie gently. "...Find out if you were okay... that's all?"

"Yeah... oh yeah." Sally laughed loudly. "Maggie and I... we're just fine... absolutely fine... isn't that right babe?"

Maggie smiled and nodded... and then... slowly... gradually... got to her feet.

"Here..." Maggie whispered calmly in Susie's direction. "... Sit down here... please... I'll go to the house and make us all a brew."

Sally didn't argue she just looked away along the beach in the opposite direction from where Susie had appeared. Susie slumped down in the chair exactly as she'd been told and tried with some difficulty to grab her breath.

"I don't understand Sal?" Susie said eventually. "…Why you ended up so bitter… why you never contacted us and let us know you were alive… that's the least you could have done?"

"Oh really…" Sally answered. "… You can't understand… well that's hardly surprising… is it… for Christ's sake… what would you know?"

"I know that we've all thought about you… every single day." Susie insisted. "… And wondered what the heck had happened to you?"

"I doubt it…" Sal growled. "… Let's face it… dad was a psychopath and mum only had time for one of us Susie… and it wasn't me?"

"That's not true." Susie emphasized trying her best to sound sincere. "… You guys might not have got along very well… but she loved you just the same… despite everything else."

"No she didn't." Sal snarled. "… That's crap… and you know it. I've no regrets… none… whatsoever. I didn't owe any of you anything… and I still don't. So as far as I'm concerned you can all go to hell."

"Well that's sad…" Susie whispered. "…Really sad… and I'm sorry you feel that way… I am honestly."

"You needn't." Sal smiled. "… Because I'm happy… happier than I've ever been. I've got a partner that loves me and takes care of me and I've a son that worships me and who would do anything for me to make sure I'm okay."

"You've a son...?" Susie gulped. "... I'd no idea?"

"No... of course not." Said Sally. "... Why would you?"

"What's his name...?" Susie asked.

"What's it to you...?" Sally croaked.

"I'm interested." Susie insisted. "... I've suddenly got a nephew I never knew existed... and I want to know all about him... everything... is that too much to ask?"

"Rory..." Said Sally proudly. "... His names Rory... and... he looks just like his father!"

"And can I see him?" Asked Susie immediately. "... This new nephew of mine."

"No!" Sal answered defiantly. "No you can't... he's down in the country for a while... on business... but if you want... I'll show you a photograph of him?"

"Yes... please." Susie smiled. "...I'd like that."

Sally dug deep into her pocket and pulled out a recent photo of her beloved son. She held it very carefully, desperate not to crease it or put any grubby finger marks across his rugged handsome features. She loved the man dearly... it was obvious... and when eventually Susie saw Rory's face... she realized why.

He was the spitting image of Susie's own precious son… of Billy!

To find a truer likeness would have been impossible.

And as Susie suddenly realized… that could mean only one thing!

"Go on then…" Sally demanded. "… Tell me… who does he look like… can you guess who Rory's father is… or do I have to spell it out for you?"

Susie had no intention of antagonizing the situation any further than it already was… although instinctively… she knew the answer to the question. Instead she decided to move the spotlight back on to herself avoiding any need to speculate on Rory's paternity.

"I've got a son as well." Susie declared excitedly. "… He's about the same age."

"Oh yeah…" Sally agreed. "… That's right… you were pregnant with Jerry before I left."

"I was." Said Susie more than happy to change the tone of the conversation. "… And you've never met him either… have you Sally? … And before you ask me… his name is Billy!"

"Men!" Shouted Sal suddenly. "…They're all bastards… aren't they… don't you think?"

"Not all of them." Susie interjected rapidly.

"Oh yeah they are." Sal insisted. "I mean… it didn't take me long to get Jerry into bed… did it? And you were five months pregnant for Christ's sake… does that bother you Susie… does it?"

Susie didn't answer.

"It would me…" Sally growled. "And you know what Sis… it wasn't hard. I had him eating out of my hand and before you know it… he was begging for it. And I've got to tell you… I gave it to him good and proper."

Sally waited anxiously for Susie's reaction… but… Susie had played the game lots of times before… many, many years ago… and now she was older and wiser and there was nothing that Sal could say about Jerry… that Susie didn't already know.

It was ancient history… and as far as Susie was concerned… water under the bridge.

"Okay then…" Said Sal ominously. "… If that doesn't bother you… and it obviously doesn't… I'll tell you something you don't know shall I… I'll tell you about that last night on the West Pennine Moors… and what happened between me and Tom Smith… do you want to know?"

"Of course…" Whispered Susie. "… You know I do."

"Well…" Insisted Sal. "Tom had given me a stash of goodies to go up there in the first place… and I was leaving the day after… I'd made arrangements with

Maggie... so I thought what the hell... I can handle him... no problem... I'll go... see what else I could get my hands on!"

"But...?" Said Susie. "... It sounds like there's a but coming?"

"Not really..." Sal sighed. "... Although he was waiting for me... and obviously... he had made plans."

"Go on..." Said Susie eagerly.

"He wasn't the only one." Sal confessed. "I'd also taken something with me... something I'd bought several months earlier... a drug."

"Yeah...?" Susie gasped.

"Oh yeah..." Said Sal. "Fluitrazepam... anyway that's what we called it back in the seventies. It has a different name now of course... most people would recognize the substance as Rohypnol!"

"I've heard of it." Said Susie. "... The date rape drug?"

"If you like..." Said Sal dismissively. "...Although as far as I was concerned... it was just protection... that's all... or so I thought!"

"Carry on..." Said Susie sounding more and more apprehensive as the conversation progressed. "...Please..."

"Well... he gave me a tour of the house." Sal announced. "... And then... when I was ready I spiked his drink… but it wasn't enough… not enough to knock him out completely anyway and whilst I was ransacking the house to try and find more loot… he must have come round. He must have… because when I went back to where I'd left him… suddenly… he wasn't there!"

"And then…?" Said Susie.

"And then he jumped out behind me." Said Sally anxiously. "… He pinned me down on the floor and all the time he was clawing at me and punching me until in the end… I just couldn't resist any more…I can't remember what happened next until suddenly I came around and he was on top of me and inside me… he raped me Susie… he raped me… that bastard raped me… and there was nothing… absolutely nothing I could do to stop him."

"I'm sorry…" Said Susie. "…I'm really sorry."

"Don't be…" Said Sal angrily. "…I had it coming."

"No you didn't." Said Susie supportively. "… How could you?"

"Because I had… okay." Sal snapped. "… I'd done some really bad things Susie… its all I deserved."

"So what happened then?" Asked Susie carefully. "… After he raped you?"

"I pretended…" Said Sal. "…You know… played him along… acted like none of it mattered. If I hadn't… I didn't know what he might do. I was frightened for my life. And then eventually when he lay back and started to doze off... I got him another drink... only this time... I laced it good and proper."

"And... he went to sleep again...?" Asked Susie.

"Oh yeah..." Said Susie. "He went off big time then."

"So what did you do?"

"I was tempted to finish him off... there and then... stove his head in maybe." Sal announced. "...But it wouldn't have helped... it was too late for that... the deed was done. So I hid some of my clothing in the house and in the garage... like he might have done if he'd killed me... I knew they'd come looking for me... and he'd be the prime suspect. The longer I stayed away... the more chance they'd charge him... and then... who knows... the way I reckoned... he might have even gone down for it.

I loaded up my bag with even more stuff. The house was an Aladdin's cave... I kid you not... the more I looked... the more I found."

"And then...?" Asked Susie.

"And then I ran." Said Sal. "I ran like the wind... and until today... I've never looked back."

"Obviously... " Said Susie. "... I couldn't have known any of that... could I?"

"No... how could you?" Said Sal. "But when you think about it carefully... Tom Smith was the ultimate predator... wasn't he? He had his wicked way with both of us… and I guess Susie that you're only grateful he didn't get you pregnant as well. At least you got married first proper before you had Billy… and that's something I could never do."

"That's true." Said Susie.

"But like I said before." Sally sighed loudly. "In the end… I've got everything I need… And what I don't need is you Susie or anyone else interfering with me, Maggie or Rory… you understand?"

Susie looked visibly shocked at Sal's sudden outburst.

"So just to let you know Susie… how I really feel about you." Sal insisted. "I'm going to tell you one last little story… okay?"

"Okay." Said Susie. "… If you must?"

"I do." Said Sal. "… Its important… to set the record straight."

"Go ahead." Susie muttered. "… I'm listening?"

"Okay… so don't say I didn't warn you." Sal stared at her elder sister impassively. "My story concerns your visit to Tom Smith's house several weeks before I went up there… remember?"

"How could I forget?" Said Susie slowly.

"Didn't you come back from there feeling awful… drugged even?" Asked Sal.

"Yeah…" Susie agreed. "…Damn right I did."

"So who spiked your drink Susie… any ideas?"

"Well… there was only one person who could have done it." Insisted Susie. "… And that was Tom."

"Wrong answer…" Sally glared. "…Think again?"

"You are kidding me?" Said Susie. "… You're winding me up… that's all."

"No I'm not." Said Sally. "…It was me you bitch… did you hear me… it was me!"

"What…?" Groaned Susie. "…What are you talking about… you weren't even there?"

"Too right I was." Said Sally nastily. "… I was there all along… but neither of you had the slightest inclination."

"I don't believe you." Screamed Susie. "… You always were a good liar Sal."

"Not this time." Sally gloated. "… I saw and heard everything and then eventually when you opened the patio doors to let some air in… I sneaked in and laced your brandy…Tom got it for you… didn't he… his idea of a good nightcap… at least that's what he said… it was brandy wasn't it… is that right? … And then you know what… I hid in the room there with you all night in the corner… and I saw what happened!"

So… go on then." Susie snapped. "… Do your worst… tell me what did happen after you'd drugged me and left me completely senseless… your own sister… what sort of monster are you Sal… have you ever given it a thought?"

Sally grinned. "You really want to know… don't you?"

Susie didn't answer… she didn't need to. Sally couldn't resist.

"Well I'll tell you then… shall I…" Sally sneered. "Put you out of your misery… eh?"

"Yes…" Susie snarled. "… Yes do!"

"Nothing…" Sal suddenly announced. "Tom Smith did absolutely nothing to you… he never touched you. Yes he came in during the night to look at you and stare at you with those big brown puppy dog eyes of his… but did he lay a finger on you… no… definitely not! And there I was waiting in the shadows willing him on… desperate to see you on your back and him on top of you… screwing you… just like you deserved. And did I want him to take advantage of you? … Hell yes… I wanted him to rape you Susie… do you hear… rape you… and you know why… because I hate you… I always have and I always will! And when you scarpered off the following morning and he chased you down the drive… I wanted him to catch you and beat the crap out of you. But he didn't did he, and you know why… because he loved you Susie… he did… he loved you. He had respect for you… something he didn't afford me a few weeks later… you know what… you make me sick!"

"No… " Said Susie strongly. "It doesn't make sense… it can't have happened that way… it's impossible?"

"Why? Sally insisted. "… Go on… tell me… which bit don't you understand?"

"When I got home that morning." Said Susie. "You were there already… you'd been running… remember?"

"I had." Said Sally. "I'd run all the way down off the moors… it must have taken me forty or fifty minutes at least… and I couldn't believe that I'd actually beaten you home… you must have stopped somewhere… you must have done?"

"I did." Said Susie suddenly. "I remember now… I parked up off the A6 not wanting to get back before mum and dad left for work."

"There you go then." Sally laughed hoarsely. "… Believe me now?"

"Oh yeah…" Susie sighed loudly. "I believe you… and you're absolutely right Sal… there is no hope for you and me… you've done us both a big favour and made me realize once again what things were like. I'll go now… leave you alone… and don't worry… you won't see me again…ever… I promise you that."

"Yeah… okay." Said Sally. "… That's fine with me… unless of course we decide to come back… Rory and I… and make a claim against Tom Smith. Prove Rory's paternity and all that… shouldn't be difficult these days… what with DNA and everything else… who knows… he might even take over Fred's old business because I'll tell you this… they've got some loot those Smiths… I can vouch for that."

"Well… that's a real shame." Said Susie coyly. "… But you've left it too late Sal."

"What do you mean?" Said Sally angrily. "Tom must be in charge by now… surely?"

"Not a chance." Said Susie. "… After you went missing they packed him off to Australia and no one has seen or heard from him since. But then later on Fred's business went belly up and someone else took it over… I don't know who runs it now… but is not one of the Smiths… that's for certain."

"Who cares anyway…?" Said Sally. "…We don't need their lousy money… and I think you're right… its time for you to leave."

"Yeah… I think so." Said Susie. "But please… be happy Sal… you and Maggie and Rory… and enjoy your life… what's left of it."

"We will." Sally sighed. "… And don't forget… I don't want to see you again Susie… understand?"

"Completely." Susie acknowledged her. "… It couldn't be clearer."

As Susie walked back along the beach towards the car she could see Maggie exiting the kitchen at the back of the property with a huge tray of drinks and snacks in her hands obviously unaware that Susie was leaving.

When she saw Susie she stopped dead in her tracks and smiled hopelessly… Susie smiled back at the woman and then turned away… she'd done what she could… and after that conversation… there was… she knew… no going back.

"Well…" Said John eagerly. "… How did it go?"

"It wasn't her." Susie answered. "… Shame isn't… I thought we were on to something for a little while… but you know what… I think its time we went home.

Chapter 27

Whether John Fairclough actually believed Susie's story was not Susie's main concern. But what she did need from him however was his loyalty and his promise that he would never under any circumstances mention to another living sole as to the reason for their visit to the Emerald Isle.

"It would be so upsetting John." Susie implored him. "… If Pat in particular even suspected that we'd made our trip in order to locate Sally and not invited her along… she'd be so upset."

"You needn't worry." Said John. "I have the greatest respect for both you and your family and if that's how it's got to be… then so be it."

And just to make sure that John's promise would never be forgotten Susie allowed him to wine and dine her on their last evening together in Ireland before their return to the U.K. and then subsequently accepted his offer of marriage, something she'd always planned to do if ever he'd summoned up enough courage to ask her.

Their journey back therefore was not tinged with any kind of failure or disappointment… and was in fact… just the opposite.

And at the first opportunity they called in to see Pat to give her the good news and unsurprisingly she was overjoyed.

"I've missed you Susie." Said Pat tearfully. "… But now you've given me some good news and something really special to look forward to… and I feel happy… unusually happy… and I'm not worried about Sally any more."

"Really…?" Said Susie inquisitively. "Why's that then…?"

"I don't know love." Pat smiled. "I've thought about her a lot recently… and somehow… I just know she's okay."

"Strange?" Said Susie. "… But if that's how you feel?"

"It is Susie." Pat agreed. "If she was coming back to us… she'd have made it by now."

"I think you're right mum." Said Susie.

"Yeah…" Said Pat. "And if she is alive… all I can pray for… is that she's happy."

"Me too…" Said Susie. "…Yeah… me too."

"We know… don't we Susie… you and I… she's out there somewhere… isn't she… she's just missing?"

"You're right mum." Susie agreed wholeheartedly. "… That's all it is…she's missing!"

She's Missing

K. E. Heaton

THE END

Printed in Dunstable, United Kingdom